"So you are not a f[...] ald's, am I right?"

"Yes."

"You came here with another guest?"

She hesitated, but then said, her voice so soft and throaty he had to lean down to hear her now that the music had started, "No."

Her breath was warm against his neck, and she smelled sweet. He was beginning to enjoy the mystery; it added a sense of adventure to the hunt. He turned to face her, looking down on her blue and silver brocade half mask, her hair a soft aureole of waving curls cascading down her back and over her shoulders. He picked up one rich brown tress with his gauntleted hand and kissed a curl. "All I dare to do," he murmured, seeing her eyes widen. She had lovely blue eyes, guileless and shaded by thick lashes; her lips pouted, full and pink like a rose in bloom.

"The code of chivalry," he said indicating her dress. "You deserve a knight, but a simple huntsman will have to do."

"Yes," she whispered.

"Yes. I would like to hear that word again. If I promise to behave like a gentleman, will you enter this pretty bower with me?"

She hesitated, but finally . . . "Yes."

From *Valentine Dreams,* by Donna Simpson

MY ONLY VALENTINE

Victoria Hinshaw
Julia Parks
Donna Simpson

ZEBRA BOOKS
Kensington Publishing Corp.
http://www.kensingtonbooks.com

ZEBRA BOOKS are published by

Kensington Publishing Corp.
850 Third Avenue
New York, NY I0022

All Kensington titles, imprints and distributed lines are available at special quantity discounts for bulk purchases for sales promotion, premiums, fund-raising, educational or institutional use.

Special book excerpts or customized printings can also be created to fit specific needs. For details, write or phone the office of the Kensington Special Sales Manager: Kensington Publishing Corp., 850 Third Avenue, New York, NY I0022. Attn. Special Sales Department. Phone: I-800-22I-2647.

Zebra and the Z logo Reg. U.S. Pat. & TM Off.

First Printing: January 2003
I0 9 8 7 6 5 4 3 2 I

Printed in the United States of America

CONTENTS

THE VALENTINE POEM
  by Victoria Hinshaw   7

THE UGLY DUCKLING'S VALENTINE
  by Julia Parks   87

VALENTINE DREAMS
  by Donna Simpson   163

THE VALENTINE POEM

Victoria Hinshaw

One

London, 1814

Miss Susan Kimball stood before the mirror, carefully watching her lips form the words. *"Bella mia, te amo . . . te amo, carissima mia."* A tall and haughty *conte* pulled her into his arms and ravished her with a cascade of kisses from her forehead to her throat. In her mind she could hear his sighs of love, see the depths of his passion.

She looked down at the small volume in her hand and turned the page, hoping to find more phrases of courtship. Instead, the next section was titled "Hiring a Carriage." What did she expect? She had been embellishing on the simple *te amo* in *The Language of the Italian States and Provinces: Being a Compendium for Travelers of Useful Declarations, Phrases, and Conversations Together with Days of the Year, Celebrations and Recognition of Saint's Days.* The book was dated 1788, nearly three decades ago. But it was all she had to teach herself the language of the region she most fervently wished to visit and experience in every sense of the word.

Again she peered into the looking glass, concentrating on how her lips moved as she whispered again, *"Te amo, bella mia."*

Her words turned to a grin. Why was she engaging in this fanciful nonsense? There would not be an enraptured *conte.* No one was going to murmur those melodious syllables to her, and she would never have the opportunity to say them back to the dark and rather dangerous man in her dreams. She stared into her own eyes for a moment, then stepped back from the mirror and surveyed herself, from her narrow waist to the wisp of a cap she wore on her head. No English gentleman had ever tried to convey such a message to her. What made her think some Florentine or Venetian would find her light brown hair, pulled back into a bun, or her ordinary gray eyes worthy of his admiration?

She could not help shaking her head as she stared into the glass. Somehow, she was the anomaly among her four sisters, the middle girl who never fit in. The others were beautiful, with their mother's pale blond curls and eyes as blue as the skies over the sweeping fields of their home near Salisbury. Susan took after the more sober features of her father, William Kimball, Baron Halford.

Looks were not the only quality that set her apart from her sisters. Araminta and Philadelphia, the two eldest, had long ago married and brought forth several children, for despite the extravagance of their names, they were as conventional as any women could be. They aspired to attain the lady's magazine descriptions of virtuous paragons of feminine worthiness. Susan's two younger sisters, Dianthe and Theodosia, were almost precisely the same. They would begin their quests for suitable husbands during this Season's marriage mart. Her mother had given up on Susan's prospects last Season, her third, after she irrevocably spurned the attentions of the only male to make an effort to solicit her attentions.

Susan turned away from the lackluster sight in the mirror. It was as though she received all the shares of

imagination meant for every one of her sisters and none
of the shares of good looks. Their minds were entirely
conventional; her head overflowed with dreams of ex-
citing travel, especially to the Italian peninsula. The
baroque glories of Rome, the frescoed churches of the
Medicis' city, the gondolas plying the canals of Venice
filled her mind and stirred her soul. How very ironic
that the kind of beauty an Italian admired in a female
belonged to her sisters, who longed for nothing beyond
the boundaries of London Society.

"Susan, you are not ready to go." The Dowager
Countess of Traisdel, Susan's grandmother, admonished
her from the hall. "You need your warmest pelisse."

Susan hid the book in the folds of her skirt as she
turned. "I shall be ready in a moment."

A quarter hour later, when they arrived at Renwick
House, Susan followed her grandmother out of the carriage and into the marbled foyer, where the footman
took their wraps.

"Lady Renwick will receive you in the blue room,"
the butler said, and led them up the wide white staircase.

Susan followed Lady Traisdel, determined not to say
a word when the conversation inevitably turned to the
plans for her sisters' presentations or her perceived failure to find a husband after several Seasons in town. She
ought to be accustomed to the topic by now. Every exchange since their arrival in London a week after the
New Year seemed to have centered on Why Susan Did
Not Take or How Dianthe and Theodosia are Certain to
Do Better than Susan.

She made her curtsy to Lady Renwick and sat beside
Lady Caroline, a quiet girl of nineteen years whose first
Season last year had been no better than Susan's. Caro
and Susan had entertained each other on the sidelines of
at least a dozen dance floors.

"Mama has a plan for me." Caro spoke softly to Susan alone as the older ladies exchanged exclamations on the peculiarity of the frigid weather.

"A plan? Whatever does she want you to do?" Susan well remembered how shyly Caro conducted herself in company, despite her delicate beauty and substantial dowry.

"She believes I should sing. She says my voice is my best asset and she wants me to perform. She has hired a music master to teach me, but I fear I shall never be able to overcome my nerves."

"Of course you can. You have a lovely voice." Susan glanced over at Lady Renwick, in close conversation with Grandmother. Caro's mother had a very good idea, if only Caro could gain courage.

"The music master, my lady, as you instructed." The butler spoke from the doorway, then stood aside as two men entered.

Susan's eyes widened. Both had the dark, wavy hair that might indicate an Italian heritage. Perhaps someone with whom she could try to converse, someone who could help her learn his language.

In the flurry of introductions and her attention to the fine figures both men presented, her mind raced far ahead of the moment, and she missed both their family names. What she heard was the unmistakable lilt of an Italian accent from the music master, who was called Antonio. His intriguingly handsome companion, called Gianni, bowed and met her gaze with eyes so black and sparkly she stared transfixed.

After he turned away, directing his attention to Lady Renwick, she could not tear her gaze from him. His complexion spoke of sunshine and open air, his hair of the gentle breezes of spring, his mouth of the touch of petals in the mist. The deep set of his eyes beneath a wide forehead and the smooth planes of his cheeks reminded Susan of the face of an angel carved by a master's hands.

Abruptly she remembered her grandmother and looked away from Gianni, relaxing her fingers from their white-knuckled clasp. She stole a surreptitious peek and found the dowager absorbed in Lady Renwick's exchange with Antonio.

Another quick glance revealed a look of enthrallment on Caro's face. Had her mother any idea of what this music master looked like when she arranged his visit? Or that his companion would be even more handsome?

Lady Renwick proceeded to enumerate her instructions. "Above all, Antonio, Lady Caroline must be ready to perform at least two selections at our annual Valentine Ball. You have just under four weeks to see she is perfectly prepared to enthrall our guests. I leave the choice of music to you once you have heard her voice. And, Caroline, you must overcome your shyness."

Susan watched Caro's face, a fascinating blend of wide-eyed admiration for Antonio's looks and utter terror at the prospect of singing in public.

"Susan, would you accompany Caroline and the gentlemen to the music room?" Lady Renwick waved them away.

Susan shook off her musings and quickly agreed. Now she wished she had taken more time with her hair this morning and put on a more becoming gown. She felt as tongue-tied as Caro looked.

The music room held an elegant new pianoforte, the newest and finest model Broadwood produced.

"If I may?" Antonio seated himself on the bench and struck a series of chords, as if testing the instrument. "Now, Lady Caroline, will-a you sing for me?"

If she had not felt so concerned for Caro, Susan would have laughed at the stricken look on her friend's face.

"I, ah, I do not . . ." Caro tried to mumble excuses.

Susan frowned when she saw Gianni's expression of mild amusement. "Perhaps we should stay out of her view. I am afraid she is rather bashful," she whispered.

"Va bene."

Susan led the way to the corner of the room, out of Caro's line of vision. Her heartbeat quickened as she stood beside a potted palm and fingered its fronds. There was only one piece of furniture here, a narrow settee barely wide enough to accommodate two.

Gianni bowed and waved her to a seat. Carefully, as if she might be sitting on eggs, she perched on the edge of the cushion. His gaze held hers for a moment before he seated himself beside her, their thighs almost touching.

"Signor, you said *'Va bene,'* meaning 'It is fine,' I believe?"

Gianni nodded, smiling. *"Si.* You know the Italian language?"

"No. Yes. That is, I have studied a little. But I have had no instruction." His nearness brought Susan a blush of warmth that belied the chill of the afternoon and their distance from the fireplace.

"So we will partake of *un po conversazione, per favore."*

Susan's mind went blank. Only the words *te amo* came to the fore, clearly unsuitable as a beginning topic. Not a single term could she recall. And though she copied his pronunciation, her voice sounded both thin and distinctively English. *"Si, per favore."*

"Bene. An important part of speaking is to form the words properly. Please watch my lips. *Questa e la camera musici, mi capisce?"*

She could watch his lips forever. His mouth was fascinating, enticing, beautiful. She wished he would simply continue talking so she could observe every movement of his appealing face.

He smiled widely. *"Ripeto. Questa e la camera musici, mi capisce?"*

She tried to shake off her foolish and imprudent thoughts. If she were going to learn from this man, she would have to get over staring at him like an awestruck henwit.

She straightened her back and cleared her throat. *"Questa e la camera musici? Si.* Is this the music room?"

"Molto bene." His dark eyes shone with encouragement.

She blurted out the question that had been on her mind since he walked in the door. "Do you tutor students? Could I persuade you to give me lessons, Signor Gianni?"

"I should be happy to assist you, but I insist that you call me Gianni, and for our lessons, you are Susanna."

She felt herself grinning like a ninnyhammer and diverted her eyes, trying to wipe the simpering expression from her face. She was not a silly rattlebrained miss just out of the schoolroom. She was a young lady with independent ideas and a taste for the unconventional. A smile from a handsome man should have no affect on her whatsoever.

That he had dreamy eyes, a strong face with prominent cheekbones, and a slightly hawkish nose . . . that his physique was trim and muscular, his height above average, both graceful and intensely masculine . . . that his dark hair waved into the kind of careless arrangement many men worked hours to achieve . . . that he was friendly and warm, if a bit too familiar . . . that he was all these extremely pleasing things should mean nothing. She could just as well learn her Italian from *un vecchio*, an old man.

Age and gender were superfluous to the learning process. But as long as Gianni had come along before anyone else qualified to teach her . . .

"Will you come to Halford House in Brook Street tomorrow about two in the afternoon and we can discuss terms?"

"Of course I shall be there."

Susan felt the nonsensical smile returning and quickly bit the inside of her lip to stop it. *"Domani?"*

He smiled more brightly than a dozen candles. *Si. Domani, Susanna mia."*

She forced her attention back to Caroline, who was squeaking out a few very tentative notes.

Gianni touched Susan's hand. "Do not worry. Maestro Antonio will draw her out and she will sing like an angel in a few weeks."

Lady Renwick appeared in the door, a look of vexation on her face. After watching her daughter, who stood with her back to the room, Lady Renwick came over to Susan.

Gianni stood, and Lady Renwick immediately took his place, hardly giving him a glance. "Susan, my dear, do you think it would help Caroline if you sang with her? Would that not give her confidence, if she is not alone?"

Susan had no desire to sing for anyone, particularly not at the Renwick's famous Valentine Ball. This year she did not plan to attend any balls or routs or ridottos or any other assembly, except the event her parents would give to present Dianthe and Theodosia. She was counting on talking her mother out of the money for a few of the dresses she would not need, additions to her little fund for financing her future travels.

Gianni spoke before she could think of a reply. "If you will excuse me, milady, I believe you have a very fine idea. Though I do not know Lady Caroline well, having a friend at one's side is always comforting."

Lady Renwick nodded vigorously. "Then it is decided, Susan. You do agree, do you not?"

Susan opened her mouth to object but caught Gianni's wink. Instead of declining, she found herself nodding her agreement.

Immediately, as Lady Renwick informed Maestro Antonio of the plan, Caro dashed to draw Susan into her embrace.

"Oh, thank you, dearest friend. All alone I could not squawk a single note, but together perhaps we can give a creditable performance."

Over Caroline's shoulder, Susan aimed a frown at Gianni but his only reaction was a polite bow and an appealingly crooked smile.

An hour later, Susan felt she had been put through her paces like a performing bear on a leash. Simple songs, many scales and exercises, even an aria or two tested the limits of her ability. Unlike her four sisters, Susan's voice was pitched low.

Antonio seemed satisfied. "We fix-a your lower register, burnish your mellow tone, and you girls sing like-a the cherubim from heaven. *Signorina* Caroline takes the high parts like-a the birds, soaring and lovely."

Susan thought he had a rather elevated idea of what he could do with them, but squashed her comments. Caroline was much too excited to have her aspirations doubted.

Gianni spoke to Susan out of the hearing of the others. "Would you consent to having me come to you at one? After we speak together, I can escort you here to sing and then I will accompany you home again. Is that acceptable?"

Susan nodded. "Very acceptable. In fact, I say *molto*

bene." She had feared the singing might spoil plans for her tutoring.

"*Brava, cara mia.*"

Susan began to think these singing lessons might have a beneficial effect. They would more than double the time she got to spend with Gianni.

In the carriage back to Halford House, the dowager propped her feet on a heated brick and cast a dour look at Susan. "I suppose you will have to go to Renwick House every day to practice."

"Yes, I expect so. Signor Gianni will come at one to tutor me in Italian and then he will accompany me to Caroline's lessons."

"I do not know what your mother will think of that when she arrives. Why do you wish to study Italian? My gel, you must be careful, or you will be known as a bluestocking."

Susan was well aware of the low esteem in which her grandmother held educated women. "It will help my singing. I believe we are to do something from one of Mozart's operas."

"All a hum, in my opinion. I am not convinced Elaine is doing the right thing having those foreigners around Caroline. She is more than likely to fall in love with one of those basket-scramblers."

"I will try to see she does not."

"The best thing I can say is that you might be displayed to advantage this year after all. Your mother will have enough to do bringing out your sisters."

Susan gave a little sigh. Mama was relying on her to help with the shopping, the fittings, all the thousands of little preparations to be made. She might never have time for Gianni unless she went to those singing lessons. "I hope then you will convince her the plan is to our advantage."

"We shall see." Grandmother still wore a skeptical look, but fortunately the short ride came to an end before she could delve any deeper.

Gianni accepted a glass of claret from his half brother, Richard, tenth Duke of Bainbridge, and settled into a deep leather chair in the library of his grace's Grosvenor Square town house. Richard, Gianni was quick to note, was dressed in formal court breeches. He must have been at a dinner at Carlton House with the Prince Regent.

Richard wore his sixty years well, his features still handsome, though his hair was thinning and his paunch expanded every year. The eldest of the ninth duke's children, Richard was old enough to be Gianni's father. The duke offered him a cigar, and when he shook his head, lit his own, puffing until his head was wreathed in aromatic smoke.

"Sorry to have called you here so late, John. I wanted to see you this afternoon, but it was impossible. We are waiting for dispatches from Lord Castlereagh, and we had hopes of receiving information from the continent today. But it was not to be."

"Where is he?"

"Heading for Paris, or so we all hope. I strongly suspect, however, that Napoleon has considerably more fight left than some of our allies give him credit for. We all agree *le Empereur*'s time is running out, but he will go down fighting, as long as his troops follow his orders."

"What is the consensus on timing?"

"Some say before the trees leaf out in Paris. Others predict he will fall even sooner. I personally tend toward the more pessimistic view. He has many more men left to kill on all sides, in my opinion."

Gianni bit back an epithet and took a sip of his wine before speaking. "Let us hope the world never again sees such arrogance and treachery. And what of Wellington?"

"He has his hands full in southern France. For every man who has come to hate Napoleon, there is one who just as passionately believes in his emperor and may fight to the death. I find it difficult to believe, when you think of the hardships that infernal Corsican has inflicted on his people."

"And all the people of Europe. What do you hear about the fate of the Italian states?"

"Probably the same things you hear. Most of them will probably be returned to some sort of Austrian control."

"Leaving all the truly Italian leaders in the lurch. Ah, I know!" Gianni paused, as he could see Richard was about to speak, then went on when his brother waved his hand and nodded. "I know, no one agrees on anything except opposition to Napoleon. They all revolt against the heavy taxes and the pressures of supplying more and more men to Napoleon's armies, but they disagree about everything else, especially on who could lead a united country."

The duke blew another cloud of cigar smoke. "Precisely. We have been fomenting dissent for years. You have written some of the broadsides yourself. But there is no one to lead, to bring the various elements together, from south to north. His Majesty's Government will not oppose the Austrians going back in if the various factions in Italy cannot unite."

"I greatly fear the cause is hopeless. Even here in London, amongst the musicians alone, there are as many opinions as there are instruments. That is why I need to go home and see how my mother's family fares. I have a hotheaded uncle who may be jeopardizing the whole family."

"I understand. Your mother's family must be your first concern, once you are finished with your mission here in London. You know, I suppose, that Prinny looks fondly upon your efforts on our behalf?"

"Prinny?"

"His Royal Highness has you on a list of those he wishes to reward."

"Reward? I had no idea Prinny knew anything about me or my meager efforts."

"Sometimes the Prince can surprise one with his interests and the extent of his knowledge. Other times he appears the buffoon. He plans to make you a baron—"

"What? He is going to do what?"

"I have told you that once the war is over, I will make over the estates at Upton Bassett to you, just as our father wished. Once that is accomplished, then the Prince will name you Baron Stansberry of Upton Bassett."

"I cannot believe it."

"He has already created numerous new peers this year and plans to name many more. Most of you have been involved in the war effort."

"But I have done so little. My information has been of little importance—the intrigues of feuding secret societies and petty uprisings, all leading nowhere. Surely this pales in comparison with the contributions of true fighters."

"John, pardon me if I repeat myself for the hundredth time. Father knew you had more skills than being cannon fodder. He was entirely correct in directing you to provide information for the foreign office and link up with Italians in England. You have been reliable, honest to a fault, and exceptional in evaluating information. Lord Castlereagh has commended you. Frankly, I am tired of providing this lecture every other month to reassure you of your usefulness."

"I apologize, Richard. It is hard for me to consider my work as valuable, as you well know."

"As Prinny would say, stubble it, John. You have given many years of your young life in the service of the realm. It will soon be time for you to return to your true role, as a son of the ninth duke of Bainbridge. You may take a place in Parliament, marry, and sire many children. And, God willing, in the years of peace to come, take your growing family to Tuscany whenever you wish."

Gianni shook his head. "I fear I sound ungrateful for your support. That is not my intention. You have been the kindest and most generous of brothers, and I know your advice to the government has been highly valuable. If I have made any contribution at all, it is a small one, though I am happy to have done so. I suppose it is a rare man who finds employment sharing bottles of wine with itinerant violinists or squiring aspiring sopranos to meet their fellow countrymen. Associating with the Italian community in London is anything but a hardship."

"Your skill in drawing out information has given us valuable insights, so do not pretend it is all drinking and carousing. For the moment, we need you to continue your work here. I expect you will be able to go to Tuscany within the year, but not quite yet."

Gianni shrugged. "I was hoping the situation would be different, but I am sure you are correct that old Nappy has quite a bit of fight left in him before he either gives up or is overthrown."

Two more glasses of claret and an hour later, Gianni wished his brother a good night and refused a lift to the fringes of his neighborhood in one of the duke's equipages. He needed the walk to clear his head. The frosty wind bit into his neck and turned his ears to ice. He drew his muffler higher and tighter and tried to think of the summer sun and warm breezes at the DiFerrante estate near Siena. Perhaps he could be there by harvest, if indeed there would be any harvest this year.

The vineyards that produced the deep red grapes he had known as a child might have been entirely destroyed by the various revolts of the last years. What few messages he had from his relatives had never mentioned the status of the land. No, he would remember the hillsides as they had once been, covered with bountiful vines soaking up the rays from above and the nutrients from the rocky loam below. This was the scene he wished to describe to Miss Kimball, the scene he might someday show her.

But perhaps not. For eight years now, he had been carrying on this masquerade. Since becoming Gianni DiFerrante, he had no contact with young ladies of the *ton,* no experience dancing attendance upon the type of female the duke expected him to marry. Miss Kimball was a most fetching miss. Perhaps she would, however unknowingly, teach him all he had forgotten about proper deportment.

While he waited for the end of his government service, while he waited to go back to Italy, Miss Kimball's company was a welcome diversion indeed.

TWO

Susan spent the morning rushing back and forth between the clothespress in her bedchamber and the table in the small salon where she studied her books on Italy, a room she secretly called her *sala Italiana*. Uncharacteristically, she could not decide whether she should perfect every detail of her ensemble or cram her head with more words in the Italian language. What did one wear on a frosty morning to practice language skills? None of her gowns seemed suitable. And should she not have a list of words ready to fill her attempts at conversation?

After changing her dress three times in as many hours, she managed to forget half the terms on the lists she compiled, and her nerves were stretched as taut as the wires on the pianoforte. She told herself she must be merely tense in anticipation of the lessons for which she had long yearned; certainly her nervousness had nothing to do with the good looks and charm of the teacher.

As the appointed hour approached, Susan tried to sit quietly and stitch beside the fire in the drawing room. The dowager observed her, a frown of disapproval pinching her thin face. "Susan, when your tutor arrives, I trust you will find some place to put him where I will not be disturbed. I deem chatter in foreign tongues to be most annoying."

"Then should I take him to the small salon?" Susan held her breath for the answer.

"Anywhere out of my hearing. I trust I can count on your good behavior."

"Why, Grandmother!"

"One never knows what to expect from these foreigners."

Susan bit back her response and quickly left to order a fire lit in her *sala*. Best to stay out of her grandmother's sight, in case Lady Traisdel changed her mind.

When Gianni arrived, Susan met him in the foyer and led him directly up to her hideaway.

His smile lit the room as no fire could as he examined the prints she had placed on the walls. "The ruins in Roma. Very good. *Molto bene.* How did you become interested in *Italia,* Susanna *mia?*"

"I have always enjoyed reading about beautiful places. I am interested in the Roman Empire and in the artists of the Renaissance. And who would not want to see the canals and gondolas of Venice?"

"You read a great deal?"

"Yes, I love to lose myself in stories, though sometimes my own imagination is more lively than the stories." In a corner of her mind, she observed her conversation as if from a distance. How was it she felt on edge and at the same time could speak with him easily, as if they were old friends?

He turned away from the prints and favored her with a wink. "You are extraordinary. I thought young ladies thought only of finding themselves an eligible match."

"Oh, I will probably never marry. Not to say that I would not like to find a loving husband. But I have had several Seasons and I did not take, as they say. My mother says I am not conventional enough, that I do not . . . Oh, this is wasting our time. Tell me where in Italy you lived, if you please." She felt a blush rise on her cheeks. Their conversation felt much too familiar for their two days of acquaintance. She should not talk to him about personal matters.

"I was born in Tuscany."

"So you lived in Florence—that is, Firenze?

"No, I did not. My family lived south of there, near Siena."

"Tell me about your home."

"I was very little when I lived there, so I have just a few impressions in my head. The city is built of stone that turns pink in the sunlight. The streets are very narrow, twist and turn, in the ancient fashion. I shall bring you some prints of Siena. You can see for yourself."

"That would be kind of you." She sat at the table before her knees gave way beneath her. "Please sit down, *signor.*"

"Remember, here I am Gianni and you are Susanna."

"Susanna. I like that! I have always wondered why my mother chose such a plain name as Susan for me. My sisters all have quite unusual and fanciful names. I am simply Susan."

"Susan is a lovely name, perhaps my favorite. I am giving it just a touch of Italian, Susanna *mia.* Now, what do you want to learn?"

She drew a deep breath. "If I am to travel, I need to speak to coach drivers, managers of inns and hotels, shopkeepers, merchants, to ask directions."

"*Bene.* Good. *Avanti, per favore.*"

"Forward, please."

"*Molto bene.* First we learn to count. *Uno, due, tre, quattro . . .*"

As the lesson proceeded, Susan concentrated with every fiber of her being. She wanted to please Gianni, to win a flash of his smile when she responded correctly. Numbers, then days of the week, seasons, and colors. "Some of the colors are easy. *Verde* is verdant green, *azzurro* is azure blue, black is *nero,* who had a black heart. But how will I remember white, *bianc*o, or brown, *marrone?"*

"You must use the words over and over again." Gianni checked the clock. "The hour has sped by, Susanna *mia.*"

Susan was amazed and disappointed at how quickly the time had passed.

Gianni continued. "We have one more thing for today, learning a few parts of the body. The heart is masculine. *Il cuore,* the heart. But the face, *la faccia,* is feminine."

"I do not understand. That is, I understand the words but not why they are masculine or feminine. Women have hearts. Men have faces." All afternoon she had admired the arch of his dark brows, his large, expressive eyes, high cheekbones tinged with color.

"I do not know the answer, *bella mia. Il curore della femma. La faccia del 'uommo.*"

"The heart of a woman. The face of a man. *Il curore della femma,*" she repeated.

"Not quite, Susanna *mia.* Watch my lips."

As if she could stop looking at his mouth. Or listening to his mellow voice.

He spoke slowly and distinctly. *"Il curore della femma."*

She nodded and tried again, forming her lips exactly as he had. *"Il curore della femma."*

"Brava! We will have to work more on the genders in the language, *cara mia.* Eventually you will find it simple and natural. Now we must hurry if we are to be on time for your singing practice."

"One question, Gianni. You speak perfect English, without a trace of an accent. How did you learn to speak so well?" The question had been lingering at the edge of her consciousness all day.

"I have lived in England since I was a boy. I am half English, half Italian. I had my schooling here."

"Ah, that explains everything." Except, she thought, how she had become enchanted by his charm, captivated by his combination of kindness and humor.

"A domani, Susanna?"

"Si. Until tomorrow. *A Domani,* Gianni."

"Now, *piu rapido, cara mia.* We must hurry."

Susan wondered how her heart could keep from bursting with delight.

The chilly hall had only one fireplace around which about thirty people stood. Others, dressed in their outdoor wraps, sat in chairs placed in crooked rows. The voices of a hundred people competed with the tuning of several dozen instruments at the front of the room. The conversations were conducted entirely in rapid Italian, mostly unintelligible to Susan, spoken too fast and often in dialects or with accents she could not make out.

Gianni waved at several people, then drew up chairs for Susan and Caro within reach of the fire's warmth. "If you will wait here, I see some people I must speak with. Excuse me for a moment."

Antonio said, "I will see when they are to start."

Alone with Caro, Susan looked around the room. It was unlike any opera performance she attended before—no stage, no curtain, no scenery. Many people were carrying musical instruments and in one corner of the room, several were playing random bits of music, some phrases repeated over and over.

"An informal performance," Caro said. "I do not know what they meant."

"Nor do I. It is all new to me. Gianni said it would be like a rehearsal with an audience."

Susan watched Gianni join a cluster of men in a shadowed corner of the room. They bent their heads together, as if they were discussing secrets, though in the noise of the room, no one three feet removed could have heard a word. When he moved away from them, he was quickly drawn into another group, this one with several women, one of whom seemed to be kissing his ear—either that or whispering with her lips practically touching him.

"Obviously most of the people here are Italians and probably many are also musicians."

"And artists. Tonio told me Signor Podesti, who painted my sister last year, might be here."

More people, crowds of them, entered the hall with accompanying gusts of chilly air. Susan wished she had her muff of warm beaver fur in which to cram her hands, but Gianni had cautioned her to dress simply, not as if she were going to a real theatrical performance.

A tall man with long white hair, wildly disarrayed, approached the area where the musicians were playing their raucous practice cacophony. Suddenly people began to take their seats and the room quieted.

Tonio sat down beside Caro and Susan. "They begin in a few moments."

Still in the far corner, Gianni's back was turned to most of the room as he listened to a man speak. Susan wondered what he had to say to or hear from so many people. When he started back toward their chairs, he was stopped again by an old man whose urgency was evident in his every move. He looked to be near tears as he grasped Gianni's arm and poured out his words. Gianni nodded several times, then appeared to reassure the old man, patting his shoulder and speaking quickly. With a handshake, they parted, and Gianni slipped into his chair beside Susan just as the conductor raised his baton before the musicians gathered at the front of the room.

"Scusi," he whispered.

Susan smiled and nodded. Anything she might have said would have been lost in the opening chords. From that moment on, she found herself lost in the music, entranced by the magnificence of the singing, the intimacy of the setting, the enthusiasm of the audience. As a language lesson, however, she found it frustrating. The sung language was even harder to follow. Yet she would have gladly stayed here forever, listening to these lovely voices and fine orchestra.

When the act ended to fervent applause, Gianni leaned toward her and spoke softly. "Your face tells me you know how exceptional this is. The popular acclaim for Madame Ponicelli's voice is well deserved."

"I cannot believe how much more I like this than the theater, though I admit I miss the costumes. The audience is much better behaved than in the opera house. Here they are truly listening. There they are busy looking at each other and criticizing their ornamentation and their trimmings. Gianni, I wish all performances could be more like this."

"But the singers and musicians will receive hardly anything. As you can see from the audience, few people here have much money to give. But even a little is better than nothing. As long as the King's Theatre is closed, many of these players have no income."

When the plate was passed for contributions, Susan emptied her reticule and gave all the coins she possessed.

Gianni excused himself again and seemed eager to talk with several men.

"Sometimes I think he knows everyone in London—that is, everyone like us from Italy."

When the performance resumed, Susan watched Gianni. He seemed to sway with the music. He held his eyes blissfully closed. Compared to most of the people here, he was fashionably dressed. Though not wearing a coat from a first-rate tailor, he was respectable enough for a man with no visible means of support other than her small payments.

She admitted her insatiable curiosity about him could not be justified by some notion of becoming better acquainted with a tutor. Her feelings ran deeper, much deeper.

Gianni led Susan, Lady Caroline, and Antonio through Bainbridge House, from the imposing marble entrance hall to his brother's picture gallery, a long narrow room where most of the renowned Bainbridge collection hung. Spending every afternoon of the last week answering Miss Kimball's questions about Italy inspired him to bring her here to view the wonders of Italian art. He was intimately familiar with every piece. Most of the collection had been assembled by his father, the ninth duke, and was currently the property of his half brother, the tenth duke. But he certainly did not intend to tell Susan, nor would he allow Antonio or Lady Caroline to know of his dual identity. He had worked too hard to keep the two parts of his life separate to let the truth seep out now.

"How did you get permission for us to visit the duke's collection?" Susan asked as they entered the gallery.

"I asked, Susanna *mia*. The duke is happy to have people enjoy his collection."

"But how do you know him?"

"Ah, my curious one, I have talked with the duke about his pictures and even advised him when he made a purchase at an auction last year." Nothing he said was untrue. But it was only a small part of the story.

He gestured to a small painting of the madonna and

child to the left of the entrance. "This may be the most precious work in the entire collection, by Sandro Botticelli, master of fifteenth century Florentine painting."

The four gathered around the panel, which glowed in the reduced light of the gallery.

"She has a lovely face," Susan breathed.

"The painting gives you the ideal of beauty of his day. Notice both the child and mother have light golden hair."

"And the palest ivory skin," Susan added.

"Precisely. These were highly prized attributes and probably not very common in Tuscany in those days."

"She looks more like an English girl."

"And note the little bow mouth and pale eyes, also probably not typical of Florentine women. Botticelli painted this model many times over. Most experts believe even though she was a real person, he idealized her and made her perfect in painting after painting, whether as the Roman goddess of love or as the Holy Virgin. Her skin color is luminous and its beauty is enhanced by the glowing red velvet of her gown."

Antonio peered at the painting, then turned to Caroline. "Miss Renwick, I think-a the Madonna resembles you. Her mouth, her cheeks."

Gianni watched Caro blush and look down shyly. Unless he was entirely mistaken, which in matters concerning the affections of young ladies he rarely was, he recognized the shy admiration of a girl discovering her first twinges of love. Lady Renwick had no idea what she was doing allowing her daughter to spend time with Antonio.

Gianni walked on to the next painting, the first of several massive canvases hanging side by side. "The present duke's father acquired four paintings by Giovanni Antonio Canal, known as Canaletto, when he was on his grand tour. The ninth duke loved Italy and spent a great deal of time there."

Gianni motioned to them to come close to the painting. "Canaletto painted these huge canvases in minute detail. When you stand back and regard them from afar, you see the sweep of the sky, the sea, the buildings of Venice, the churches, the Doge's Palace. In every picture, you also find the ordinary people of the city." He pointed at the picture's foreground. "Here are two fisherman, dragging their nets from their skiff, and over there are two dogs fighting over a morsel of food."

Susan peered at the small figures. "The detail is amazing."

"Yes." Gianni put his arm around her shoulders and pointed at one edge of the painting. "Look at that woman in the window holding the baby. She is as well painted as the figure of the Doge himself."

They stood in silence for a moment, then moved to the next vast painting.

"The duke bought this Canaletto in London, showing the view from gardens along the Thames."

"Why, there is St. Paul's," Caro said.

"Yes, and in the corner of the garden, a man works with a rake, oblivious to the great church across the river."

Slowly they worked their way down the gallery, exclaiming about each painting in its turn. Gianni was not surprised when eventually Antonio and Lady Caroline sat down on a bench at the end of the room. Susan, however, showed no sign of flagging in her enthusiasm for every canvas.

He smiled into her upturned face and moved to the next painting. "This is by Antonio Guardi, a great Venetian who became a friend of the duke, it is said. It shows Santa Maria Della Salute in Venice. See how Guardi and Canaletto used differing techniques. Guardi uses a buildup of paint to show the intricate shapes and moldings on the church. The amount of paint itself creates shadows that emphasize the detail."

"You know so much about these techniques. Do you paint or draw?" Susan asked.

Gianni laughed. "No, I have no talents whatsoever. I am not musical, nor am I artistic. I must rely on my wits to see me through this life."

"Then you will be a very successful man, I predict."

Gianni squeezed her hand and tucked under his elbow. "You tease me, *carissima mia.*"

She shook her head. "Not at all. You are very clever."

"I thank you, but your praise is undeserved."

"Nonsense! You explain everything so well. I know little about art, but I love these views, especially the pictures of Italy," Susan said. "They make me want to travel there even more."

"So that is your dream?"

"Yes, I want make plans to go as soon as I can. Perhaps you might help me?"

"It would be my pleasure, Susanna *mia.*"

She smiled at him, a smile of such luminous beauty he could only compare her to the beautiful Tiepolo Venus that hung in the duke's study, where he could not take her today. "What can I do?"

"I need to find a lady or a family that plans to go to Italy in the next year. I wish to become a companion."

He could hardly believe what he heard. "You? You wish to become a companion to some eccentric old person or end up caring for someone's children?"

"Ah, Signor DiFerrante, I wish there was another way, but I have four sisters and two brothers. None of us but George, my oldest brother, will have more than a small legacy. Mine will be barely large enough to live on; certainly not enough to allow me to travel."

"But you intend to marry, do you not?"

"I believe most fellows prefer more biddable young ladies with a larger dowry than I have. And who are prettier and more accomplished."

"Prettier? I find that hard to fathom. As for accomplishments, does a lively intelligence not count for anything?"

"Indeed it may be a disadvantage, if of course one can be said to have any worthwhile mental attributes at all."

"You must not tease me, Susanna *mia*. It is not kind to tell fibs to a poor fellow like me, who cannot mount the defense of your charms that is required by your exaggerated self-criticism."

"Now you are the one who is teasing."

"We shall agree to disagree." Gianni gave her a little bow and crossed the gallery to a lovely statue of Daphne fleeing from Apollo.

"I know this story," Susan said. "Look at her arms. She is turning into a tree."

"Esattamente. Exactly."

They sat on a brocade bench and stared at the polished white marble.

Susan gave a little sigh. "I wonder if she was happy to be turned into a laurel tree rather than giving in to Apollo."

"On that I choose not to speculate."

"Very wise."

Gianni swung his feet to the other side of the bench. "If you turn, you will find Mercury behind you."

She followed his instructions. He was rewarded by a little gasp as she took in the elegant stance of the polished bronze sculpture. Mercury was balanced on one foot, caught in midstep, his arm raising his caduceus high in the air.

Gianni nodded. "Not an uncomplicated achievement

for a sculptor, to balance the figure that way. It is only about one hundred years old, the messenger of the gods, with his winged feet. Also the patron of all knaves and rascals, I believe."

"Vagabonds, rogues, and thieves, as I recall."

Gianni joined her in laughter. He could not remember enjoying an afternoon more.

After dinner, Susan sat in the gold salon, her book of Italian grammar in her hands. Instead of looking at the pages, studying new words and formulating new questions to ask of Gianni, she was lost in dreamy thoughts of the way he explored that vast landscape of Canaletto.

His masculine beauty and grace moved her in ways she could not fathom. His gesturing hands moved in flowing circles, not in short, choppy motions. She had stared more at his long and elegant fingers than at the painting.

He was himself a work of art, dark long lashes and a broad grin, a full lower lip. His eyes, bright with points of light, gave meaning to the term flashing eyes. A curl carelessly drooped over his forehead. Susan had never had this strong a reaction to a man. Or to a work of art.

The dowager, seated next to the fire, looked up from her embroidery. "Where did you go today, Susan? You have not told me of your afternoon."

"Lady Caro and I went to Bainbridge House to see the duke's paintings."

Lady Traisdel was instantly alert. "The Duke of Bainbridge? How extraordinary. Is he a friend of the Renwicks?"

"The duke was not there. Signor DiFerrante took us. He said he had given advice to the duke on the purchase of artwork, so he is allowed into the gallery."

"I am stunned. The duke is a very important personage, a close friend of the Prince Regent, I hear."

"He has a fine collection of paintings. We had a very interesting afternoon."

"I am glad you enjoyed yourself." The dowager bent her head again to her silks.

What would Grandmama think if Susan told her about the way Caro and Antonio had flirted with one another? Or worse, if Susan admitted her attraction for the handsome Gianni? Obviously she could say nothing.

There were some things about Gianni that she wondered about. He spoke English with the accents of the highest circles. He had no profession, no obvious means of financial support. How did he make his living? Perhaps his advice on buying pictures brought him funds.

The more she thought about Gianni, the more Susan felt she was missing some essential facts. Who was he really?

Oh, nonsense! She was obviously thinking he must be someone special because she was so agitated by thoughts of him. *Don't be a peagoose, Susan! He is exactly what he says he is, a poor Italian exiled from his home country and stuck here in frigid London.*

Just because she went all soft inside whenever she was near him did not mean he was anything more than a very handsome and charming fellow—and probably one who thought she was an heiress just like Caro, no matter what she had said. He would know the truth soon enough, when Mama and her younger sisters arrived. Not one of the Kimball girls had more than a tiny portion, not enough to attract the most desperate of fortune hunters.

She might as well face the facts. His charming attention to her would end as soon as she stopped paying him for lessons in speaking Italian.

Three

"Oh, you are such a flatterer." Madama Poldi extended a plump hand, letting her beringed fingers caress Gianni's cheek. "You could not possibly care about what my brother writes. He is nothing more than a *bambino.*"

Gianni grinned and pressed her hand to his lips. *A* bambino *intricately involved in the machinations of the* carbonieri, *a* bambino *who was probably one of the masterminds among the secret societies in central Italy, a* bambino *whose words could reveal whether any of the attempts at unity might succeed.*

"I shall pour the *vino,* Gianni, and we will talk. Don't you long for the sunshine of Roma, the warm breezes? I shiver all day and all night in this wretched cold."

If anything, he thought, her room was too warm. Airless and stuffy. "Of course. To see the seven hills, to see the poppies on the roadside. I long to go home."

He could not tell whether the tear that ran down her cheek was real emotion or a trick summoned from her old days singing tragic arias.

She waved her handkerchief dramatically. "In my father's grove were hundreds of olive trees . . ."

Gianni had listened before to this recital of the brilliance of Madama's childhood home. It would lead slowly into the story of her discovery and tutelage by one of the last century's most famous impresarios. After long diversions covering her splendid successes on stages throughout the Continent, she would eventually enumerate her triumphs in London, embellish reports of each of her roles, and ultimately descend into the sad ending: her health problems, the loss of her voice, and the eventual livelihood she found designing and sewing costumes for the productions in which she once starred. Gianni was confident every one of the thousands of Italian exiles in London knew this story, most of them hearing it directly from her lips.

He did not halt her performance. The last time he visited here, Gianni had tried to stem the tide of words, half Italian, half English, and found himself suddenly entwined in her arms. Extricating himself had been difficult and time consuming. This morning, instead, he armed himself with a suitably sympathetic expression and murmured an occasional word of condolence when she paused to wipe her eyes.

As he listened with half an ear, he ran over the gist of the dozen relevant bits of information he had received in the last three days. When he added together the gossip, the word of a recent arrival from Milan and the newspaper accounts, the outcome was disappointing, if predictable. No leader had come forth to bring unity to all the factions on the Italian peninsula. A gloomy conclusion, but not unexpected.

Madama reached the decline of her once vibrant soprano. "They pushed me too hard, too soon. Too many performances, too many demands . . ."

Gianni mumbled some words of understanding. He suspected the real problems were too many late nights with too many men and too much wine. It was a trap many of his talented countrywomen fell into in London. Probably in Paris, Berlin, and Saint Petersburg as well.

He patted her hand as she came to the poignant ending,

the strained eyesight, the pricked fingers, the backaches from hunching over the bead box.

Time now, he thought, *to get to the business at hand.*

"Madama, the magnificence of your voice makes me yearn to hear more. Now you can read your brother's letter. Do not deny me the splendor of your tones."

"Ah, Gianni, could you not spare me the tiniest embrace?"

He pretended to bristle. "You naughty puss! You know one tiny embrace would never be enough. I would be here all afternoon, all evening. I would be unable to leave, and that is impossible, *dolce mia.* You are wicked to tempt me so."

"Pooh. You do not fool me, Gianni. I know I am too old and fat for a beautiful young Apollo like you. I know you, flattering one. You like the younger girls, the dancers."

"But no one has your voice, Madama."

"Not much of it is left, but some say the tones are as true as ever."

"Indeed they are. I close my eyes and you read. The words do not matter, just the beauty of your tones."

He shut his eyes and leaned back against the shabby velvet pillow. Would she read or would she crawl on top of him and try a seduction?

With only a moment's hesitation, she unfolded the paper and began to read, drawing out each vowel and embellishing each sentence as though she performed an aria. The first words concerned her family, the health of her uncle, their concern for her. Gianni truly did enjoy the lovely timbre of her voice. Madama's talents had been renowned in many opera houses and her performances well attended twenty years ago. He was fond of the woman, though hardly interested in her romantic advances.

Eventually she reached the political news, and stopped as soon as she got to what he wanted to hear. "This part is about all the arguments. You will be bored."

"Not a bit of it. Please go on. I remember how your brother builds to his finale and how you empathize with his every emotion."

She picked up the last page of the letter, and he lay back again and closed his eyes. The news was even worse than he expected. Neither Poldi nor any of his compatriots had the intention of throwing their support to unity, mired as they were in local arguments, petty disputes, and lack of vision. For the foreseeable future, the movement for Italian unity was doomed.

A footman in Renwick livery carried a second large branch of candles into the music room and set it on a gilded table before a tall mirror.

"That should brighten things up." Caro repositioned the candlesticks slightly.

"There has been no sun for days." Susan watched the men in the street shoveling icy crusts of snow into a cart. "But you, my dear friend, you have improved more than I could imagine."

"Oh, do you think so?" Caro's face glowed with excitement. "Tonio has been so helpful. Without him, I would be lost."

Gianni and Antonio had left the room a few minutes before, after an hour's practice ostensibly to smoke a cigar, but Susan suspected, even more likely to have a few sips of wine. "When they return, we should do the Seraphim one more time. If you listen as well as sing, you will hear the progress."

"That is difficult, but I shall try. My nerves are still on edge about our performance, but I think I will be able to get through it if we keep practicing. I will look only at you and Tonio, not at the audience."

Susan knew the source of Caro's growing confidence; the situation was sadly obvious. Lady Caroline Renwick, heiress to a handsome fortune, was falling in love with Antonio Scorsi, a penniless Italian music master. His tutelage brought her improved techniques for breathing, for reaching and holding the highest notes, for lightening her timbre with the highest head tones. But it was her determination to please him and her romantic devotion that truly inspired her singing. Every day, Caro's hair was neatly dressed, her dresses in the first stare of fashion, her handkerchiefs doused in scent. Tonio was changing her from a shy, country miss into a polished and vivacious young lady.

All of which caused Susan to worry. Every day, she wondered if she should speak to Lady Renwick. Tonio seemed too skilled at the art of making love through his music not to have left a long trail of broken hearts behind him. What was her responsibility? Would she be doing her friend a disservice by causing her to lose her maestro, or would she be preventing a scandal if Caro tried to run off with Tonio?

She was still gazing at the street when the men returned to the room.

"Now, again-a, ladies," Tonio said, launching an arpeggio on the Broadwood. Susan stood next to Caro at the side of the pianoforte just as though they faced a roomful of people.

Gianni, their sole observer, settled across the room, the usual position from which he observed the lessons. As she and Caro sang, Susan tried not to let her gaze linger on him. She was not so far from the danger that threatened Caro. She spent an hour every day with Gianni before they came here for the singing, precious hours that she enjoyed not only for the progress she made toward speaking in Italian, but also for his companionship.

Her mother would be horrified if she knew the dowager allowed them to sit and talk together, alone in a small room. And to be honest, Susan thought, exactly what her mother feared might well be a possibility. His nearness might lead her to the very improprieties Mother would condemn, but which Susan longed to commit.

"Un piu repetito. From the beginning," Tonio said when they finished.

She glanced at Caro, whose smile glowed as she prepared to start over. Susan nodded her agreement; she felt as though she could sing this number in her sleep. She turned her gaze toward the far corner of the room.

Gianni seemed lost in thought, oblivious to the music. He had the most beautiful lips, lips whose movements she tried to imitate as they spoke. Usually his mouth was curved into a smile, but at this moment, he looked grave, almost as though the weight of the world lay on his wide shoulders. Susan knew she should try to curtail her interest in him, for her fascination could lead nowhere. Even for her, with her unconventional ideas about being independent and traveling to Italy, involvement with a poor Italian fellow was irrational in the extreme.

He shifted in his chair and met her gaze, breaking into a wide smile, his dark eyes twinkling and one eyebrow raised at an impish angle. For an instant, she lost track of where she was and almost stopped singing.

Susan borrowed the dowager's fur-lined blue velvet cape to wear to the theater. Not only was it elegant, it was warm enough to fight off the chills of the February

wind. When she asked for and received permission to
wear Lady Traisdel's cloak, she was careful to mask her
amazement that Lady Renwick had given permission
for her daughter to be escorted by Maestro Antonio and
Gianni to an evening event at the Sans-Pareil Theatre,
of all places. But as Susan correctly guessed, her grandmother considered Lady Renwick's acquiescence to be
sufficient rationale to allow Susan's participation.

As the four of them climbed down from the coach
provided by Lady Renwick, Susan was grateful for the
warmth of her outerwear for it seemed they were
stopped by more than a dozen persons as they traversed
the few feet from the street to the theater entrance. All
seemed determined to speak to Gianni, their words in-
coherent to Susan but their urgency clear in their
demeanor. As they went up the stairs to their box, a
young woman with rouged cheeks and heavily outlined
eyes clutched at his arm and pleaded with him. He nodded and patted her hand.

"I am sorry, *carissima mia*," he whispered to Susan
as he held her chair and draped her cloak across its
back. "I have several people to whom I must speak. I
shall return in a few moments."

Tonio made a dismissive gesture. "Gianni, he must
talk to ever'one, ever'place. Talk, talk." He shook his
head.

Susan hardly noticed the theater's interior. Again her
brain was spinning with questions about Gianni. Despite their growing friendship and their many hours
spent together, she still felt he carried secrets he would
not share. She had considered and rejected all sorts of
explanations.

For several days, she had tortured herself with the
thought he might have a wife and family or a lover hidden away who sent emissaries to beg him to come

home. But he was too kind, too polite to conduct such devious mischief, of that she was convinced. Perhaps it was some sort of unauthorized business he conducted, though she doubted smugglers and dealers in stolen goods met in the middle of crowded halls or in front of well-attended theaters. Nor did his associates seem like they would be purveyors of the kind of artwork on which he advised that duke.

Not that all of the persons seeking his attention were male! The female on the stairs a few minutes ago looked like a lightskirt, and so had some others he had spoken with. Curse the imagination that brought her such thoughts! How could she think such a thing, that he might be some sort of a procurer? Those men were the lowest of the low, the scum of the gutters. To suppose Gianni might be one of them was unthinkable.

Though Susan was relieved when Gianni returned to the box and took his seat beside her, the evening's production failed to earn her closest attention. The dancers seemed no more than moving shapes drawing only a tiny part of her mind. The rest of her thoughts raced around the universe seeking answers to questions she could hardly compose.

Her thoughts grew darker when she noticed the girl who just stopped Gianni on the stairs. She was a dancer, clad in a filmy costume of thin fabric. Dancers, she heard, had dreadful reputations for leading young men astray.

Susan stole a look at Gianni. Unless she was completely mistaken, he hardly noticed the activity on the stage. He seemed distracted, far from the theater and lost in thought. As she watched him, he frowned and took a deep breath, an expression of sadness on his handsome face.

Obviously the comic play *The Milkmaid, or Rustic*

Lovers, was penetrating his consciousness no more than
it did hers. Susan could hear gales of laughter from the
audience at the humorous parts. Caro and Tonio seemed
entranced by the spectacle, while she and Gianni sat
soberly side by side, yet entirely alone in the crowded
theater.

It seemed like hours before the music reached its
final crescendo, the curtain fell, and the audience broke
into wild applause.

"Was that not wonderful?" Wide-eyed, Caro leaned
over to Susan, awe in her voice.

"Indeed, I have never seen such a thing," Susan
replied.

Gianni threw off his reverie. "I, for one, am looking
forward to the pantomime. I feel the need for a good
round of laughter."

Susan smiled. "I agree. Something as frivolous and
silly as possible."

When *The Magician, or The Enchanted Bird,* got
under way, Susan was not disappointed. Her smiles
turned to giggles, then into laughter she could hardly
control. When the mechanical bird flew about the stage
as if real, just out of reach of the hilariously bumbling
magician, she had to wipe tears of mirth from her eyes.

By the time the pantomime finished to uproarious
cheers, all four inhabitants of the box were weak with
laughter.

"My side aches," Caro gasped.

"Mine, too." Tonio sprawled in his chair and pretended to be overcome.

Gianni reached for Susan's hand and gave it a
squeeze, then arranged her cloak on her shoulders. The
exiting spectators were in a jaunty mood, laughter rip-
pling from one side of the stairs to the other.

Gianni handed Susan into the Renwick coach just

outside the theater. She felt relieved they had escaped the theater without further demands for Gianni's attention. His mood now seemed as jovial as Tonio's. They joined in a short chorus of a song in Italian that caused them more laughter but which they would not translate for Susan and Caro. Tonio removed the shade and blew out the single candle lighting the interior.

The darkened coach moved slowly through streets crowded with vehicles and still partially blocked by ice and snow. Antonio produced a bottle of champagne and four glasses and popped the cork with care, not spilling a drop.

Susan accepted her glass with trepidation. On previous occasions, she had never cared for the tickly liquid.

Gianni leaned close and clinked his glass against hers. *"Salute,* Susanna *mia."*

"Salute," she replied. Cautiously, she tried a tiny sip. The taste was delicious. She tipped a little more into her mouth. Even better. Its sparkle flowed down her throat and made her giggle.

As the coach lurched over a rut, Susan fell against Gianni and he put his arm around her, holding her tightly to him. She swallowed more of her champagne and held out the glass for Tonio to refill.

Again she drained the glass. Never had anything tasted so luscious. Gianni took her empty glass and set it on the floor.

In the passing light of a streetlamp, Susan saw Tonio kissing Caro. She felt as though she ought to stop them, remind them of what Lady Renwick would say if she knew how they were using her fine coach. But she did not move.

Caro seemed very happy to be kissed. Her little murmurs had the ring of delight, not opposition. Susan thought Lady Renwick was counting on her as a sort of chaperon, but her body felt too languorous to move, as though her arms and legs had turned to liquid.

"One more sip?" she asked Tonio.

Without detaching himself from Caro, Tonio handed the champagne bottle to Gianni.

"Here, *carissima mia*," he whispered, holding the bottle to her lips. Susan had never drunk from a wine bottle before. In all her twenty-two years, no one had ever expected her to indulge in such misconduct. Yet it was as effortless as sipping from a glass. The mouthful of wine went down so easily she took another.

Gianni squeezed her to him and took his own deep swig, setting the bottle beside the glasses on the floor. The coach was silent, all the outside noises faded.

Susan gazed at his face in the dim light, yearning for his lips to meet hers. Her eyes closed as if beyond her control, and her chin tipped up, waiting for the gentle touch of his mouth. It would not be her very first kiss, but the first she truly desired.

"Susanna *mia,* I should not do this." His voice was almost a groan.

"Please," she whispered.

With a tiny growl of pleasure, he brushed his lips across hers, once, twice, and again. They were feather kisses, as sweet and ephemeral as the bubbles in the champagne, as enticing as the tingle of wine spreading though her limbs, kisses so precious they stole her breath and raised all her senses to a feverous heat. Kisses so cherished she wanted more, many more, a lifetime's worth.

He tasted of champagne, and at last she knew why people loved to drink it. She felt as though she had finished an entire bottle by herself instead of just a few swallows. She wound her arms about his neck and sank back on the soft squabs, pulling him with her. She heard his little moan of pleasure when he pressed his mouth harder against hers. Their quickening breaths mingled, and she thought she might faint away with delight.

She had no awareness of the coach moving, of time passing. She knew only his body, heavy and warm pressing against her, his lips, turning hers to fire, his voice, arousing her with the treasured words she craved: "Susanna *mia, te amo.*"

Four

Susan sat at her dressing table while her maid Peg brushed her hair. With each long stroke, she let herself sink deeper into her reverie. Kissing Gianni was the most wonderful thing that had ever happened to her. He was sweet, gentle, his lips soft, his touch wonderful. She wished she could sit here forever, reliving those kisses. No! She wished she had Gianni's arms around her as they snuggled together in the chilly coach.

"Te amo, signor, caro mio. Te amo." She let the unspoken words echo in her head as she reveled in the movement of Peg's brush.

"Miss Susan?" Peg's hand was still. "Are you awake?"

"Oh, Peg. I am sorry. I was thinking of something else, far, far away."

"Can I braid now?"

"Yes. Do you have a fellow, Peg?"

The maid paused in dividing strands of Susan's long hair. With a little blush, she nodded. "Yes'm, I walk out with Fred, one of Lady Traisdel's footmen."

"Are you in love with him? Do you feel like your feet are not touching the floor when you stand next to him?"

"Oh, yes, miss. Or I wanna jump up and down like an exited pup."

"Do you feel as though your chest is collapsing inside you? And you cannot catch your breath?"

"I do. Are you in love, Miss Susan?"

"I do not know. I only know I feel very strange when I am around a certain man. Has Fred kissed you?"

"Oh, miss. I canna say." Peg could not choke back a little giggle. "When Fred kisses me, a dozen fuzzy chicks jump around inside me, flapping their wings and tickling me in a way I canna scratch."

"Yes, Peg. I know that feeling exactly. Does that mean I am in love?"

"Oooh, that I canna know. But you be careful, miss. Me mum sez menfolk take what they can get from girls who dunna keep both feet on the ground, if you take my meaning."

"Gracious, I suppose I do. Both feet." Last night she was certain neither of her slippers had touched the floor of the coach.

Susan pushed the draperies as far back from the window as they would go. Even that hardly helped the efforts of a thin sun gallantly trying to break through a haze of clouds. As she waited for Gianni to arrive for her Italian lesson, the dimness of the room reminded her of the darkness last night in the coach, of the warmth she enjoyed in Gianni's arms.

Just the thought made her weak with emotion. Now, hours later, in the light of day, how could she know what those whispered words meant? And if he loved her, what did it matter? There could be no future for the two of them. She simply had to get those thoughts out of her head or she would not be able to accomplish anything this afternoon.

He would be here any moment. She must eliminate the silly grin on her face, a grin she could not wipe away no matter how she tried. It gaped at her from every mirror she passed. Pinching her cheeks or nipping at the edge of her tongue did not seem to help. But no matter how she grinned at the lingering effects of being kissed by him, she really did not know Gianni.

Last night, before the earth-shattering events on the way home, she had watched Gianni talking to people, his discussions serious, his face often grim. She was certain, after several instances of these contacts, that he was not just a simple exile. Instead of grinning like an idiot, she should be formulating questions that would help her find out the answers.

But even as he entered the room and kissed her hand, she could not stop wishing she were back inside the coach, deep in his embrace.

"Buon giorno, bella mia." Gianni carried a package wrapped in brown paper. He set it on the table and opened it as she watched, her doubts forgotten.

"There are two prints. This is the Campo and the Palazzo Pubblico, from the thirteenth century. And this one is the Duomo, the cathedral, a triumph of Sienese Gothic architecture."

Susan gazed at the prints, her throat clogged with sudden tears. "They are beautiful," she murmured.

"They are for you to hang here, Susanna *mia,* so that you never forget Gianni. And someday, we will stand here, together in the Campo." He pointed to a spot near the center of a print. "And you will see the clearest light, and the colors, pinks and ochres glowing in rivalry with the brilliant blues of the sky."

"Grazie, Gianni."

He smiled and nodded. "You are an excellent student."

"Nonsense!"

"I have something else for you, *cara mia.* Last evening I studied the advertisements printed in the

Times. Certain phrases seem useful for persons desiring a position. Do you know them?"

"No, I have never—"

"If you want to be a governess or a companion, you must see what to say. You might be 'a young lady desirous of taking a position . . .' or 'a lady whose connections are of the first respectability.'"

"Oh my, I would not know . . ."

"Or 'a young person of respectable family who wishes for a situation to wait on a lady; she will do her best to please'?"

"Those words are in the *Times?*"

"Yes, *cara mia.* I do not think this is your future. You must get to Italy another way—perhaps with me, Susanna *mia.*"

Susan's breath caught in her throat. "What?"

Abruptly Peg burst into the room. "Miss Susan, your mama and papa have arrived with yer sisters. Mr. Gianni, Lady Traisdel sez you have to go out the back way. And quick."

Now that he sat before a fire in his brother's comfortable library, Gianni could manage a laugh, however rueful. Being rushed down the servants' stairs and ejected from Halford House without his coat, scarf, or gloves had just about done him in. Peg had sent him to the mews, where she promised to bring him his coat once she survived the initial flurry of tasks associated with the arrival of Lady Serena and her daughters.

Since the distance was not great, he had decided instead to hasten to Bainbridge House, avoiding the questions of the Halford grooms. He had not considered the treacherous footing in the cross streets, the icy mounds of snow, the glassy sheets of ice where snow had melted and refrozen several times, all negotiated while the wind tore through his flimsy jacket and nipped his ears and fingers to the bone.

Now that he was warming up, he found it quite amusing to have been the potential cause of so much trouble. Susan told him the first time he came to her house that her grandmother, however proper she claimed to be, was interested primarily in her own comfort and convenience. In sending him away so unceremoniously, the dowager was acknowledging the fact her daughter would not approve of the way she supervised Susan. Someday, when he knew her on a different level, perhaps he would have the opportunity to thank her.

Or wish her to perdition.

If he and Susan had not had all those hours alone, he never would have found himself falling in love. Or was it Lady Renwick's fault, hiring Antonio and asking him to bring along a friend?

His life might be headed in a very different direction at this moment if he had never met Miss Susan Kimball. His feelings for her required him to reveal his true identity to her before much longer. He had no idea how she would react.

Would she regard him as an imposter, devious and amoral? Or would she understand his motives and forgive him his masquerade?

He wondered if he returned to being Lord John and circulated in Society, would he remember how to behave? For eight years, he had been Gianni, free of all the constraints of the *haut ton,* free to be as outrageous as he wanted. He rarely met anyone in London's social circles. When he did and was ignored or overlooked as introductions were made, he did not mind in the least. He was, in the role he had adopted, something slightly more than a servant, but less than a man of business or a merchant. He was invisible, a part of the furniture, and so treated.

Fool! *Il sciocco!* Why was he even thinking of London Society? He had considered Miss Susan Kimball as a minor diversion while he waited for the time he could leave England. Over the weeks, he had let down his guard. The other night in the carriage, he had tossed prudence aside and let his foolish passions reign. A simple flirtation had become something else. But what? What did it mean?

That his regard for his Susanna had grown he knew well. But to think he could feel something deeper for her, something that whispered marriage, forever, family, and trouble! How very ironic the first young lady he had cared for seriously knew him as a man totally unqualified to court her. And further, as a man who had taken liberties with her she might someday regret.

As Lord John Stansberry, her mother would welcome him as a contender for her hand. He was not a peer of the realm, but he was a gentleman with a handsome income and the promise of much more to come. The Prince Regent might not come up with that barony Richard mentioned, but the duke would certainly cede the lands their father had intended for John. If he had not been engaged in this questionably valuable business here in town, he would have been living on that estate long ago. Or, if he had followed his original preference and bought a pair of colors, he might have occupied a shallow grave in Portugal.

Richard's butler entered with Gianni's coat over his arm. "Tom has returned with your things, milord." With care undeserved by the rather shabby coat, Norton draped the garment over a chair near the fire.

"Thank you, Norton. And thank Tom for me as well. I appreciate the difficulty of the retrieval."

* * *

In a silken dressing gown, Mama lounged on her chaise and surveyed her three daughters and her mother, all four sitting nearby.

Susan prayed she could rely on her grandmother not to talk about the Italian lessons or particularly about the Italian tutor and the fact they had usually been alone together. The dowager knew such an arrangement would not meet with Lady Serena's approval.

Lady Traisdel and her daughter had an interesting relationship, a combination of rampant rivalry and deep devotion. The dowager disliked arguments with her daughter about propriety. When not together, each claimed higher standards than the other. The dowager Lady Traisdel decried the slumping behavior of today's society. Lady Serena claimed morals had been much looser in the previous century, when her mother was young.

Susan heard the arguments on both sides and found no reason to choose one over the other. As far as she was concerned, both her mother and grandmother would revise their supposedly unyielding standards to fit whatever their whims dictated, as Lady Traisdel had where Gianni was concerned.

But in the field of finding matches for daughters, the dowager had a superior record, of which she reminded her daughter frequently. Lady Traisdel had landed an earl for herself. For her daughters she had secured the Baron Halford and the Viscount Randolph, Susan's uncle.

Neither of Lady Serena's eldest daughters, Araminta and Philadelphia, had married a title, though both were well fixed. Phil's husband, Mr. Clark, came from a family with a noted banking fortune. As for Susan, she had been such a disappointment to both her grandmother and mother she hardly counted in the competition.

Lady Serena sighed and drew a cashmere lap robe over her legs. "I fear I shall be chilly until June. Traveling has been a nightmare. One never knew where one might be stopped by uprooted trees, unsteady bridges, and terrible snow and ice everywhere."

"Susan, you should have seen the garden at home." Theodosia looked so young and fresh it was impossible to think she had recently climbed out of the coach weeping over the chills in her feet. "Everything was coated with frost. It was very strange."

"Hideous to me," said Dianthe. "I could barely stand to look at it."

Susan wished she could have seen it, even more like an enchanted fairyland than the view of the icy trees in the square.

"Everything has been hideous." Dianthe wrinkled her nose in distaste. "Six days on the road—nearly a week—when it usually takes three days."

"We had to get here," Lady Serena said. "Neither of you want to miss the Renwick's ball on St. Valentine's Day. I assume you are planning to attend, Susan."

"Yes. In fact I am going to sing, along with Lady Caroline. To give her confidence."

"Yes, she is a timid chit." Lady Serena repeated her deep sigh. "I suppose that is one of Elaine's schemes to bring her daughter to the attention of some eligible *parti*. Even with all her money, she was practically invisible last Season."

"We practice every day at three."

"That may not always be convenient, Susan. You may have duties here at home to help your sisters."

"Mama, I have promised Lady Renwick. I am sure

you would not want me to break that vow. After all the ball is only two weeks away."

"Sixteen days. But I suppose there is nothing to be done."

Susan clamped her lips shut. Further discussion would only lead to arguments. Any hope of continuing Italian lessons here at Halford House was futile for the moment. At least she would have her afternoons to see Gianni.

Not for a second had his words been out of her thoughts. He had asked her to come to Italy with him. But he had been teasing her, had he not? Oh, how she wished he was serious!

Five

Susan sat in her bedchamber staring at the print of Siena's Campo. She had memorized every line, every curve, every mark, but she never tired of looking at the *piazza* and thinking about Gianni walking across its broad expanse. She had brought both of the prints upstairs to hang near her dressing table. She considered it the better part of caution to bring her Italian books up as well. Mama's orders to turn out and thoroughly clean every room on the first floor had the household in an uproar. Her *sala Italiana* was scheduled to have its decor refreshed.

Susan viewed the weeks she and her grandmother spent in London as a lovely and calm interlude before the storm. Now that her mother and sisters had arrived, all efforts of the entire household were concentrated on preparing Dianthe and Theodosia for their presentations and the events of the Season. Except Papa. He spent most of his days at his club.

All five ladies of the household had schedules filled with fittings, shopping excursions, and social calls, both made and received. The list of tasks grew by the hour.

Conversation exclusively dealt with the upcoming months. The attributes of other young ladies to be presented were endlessly examined. Eligible young men, and not a few older ones, were analyzed, their fortunes assessed, their habits, good and bad, dissected. The timing of various balls, routs, and Venetian breakfasts was calculated. Certainly, Susan thought, Wellington did not hold more intense meetings to plan his battle strategy.

She was relieved her mother could not spare an hour to attend the singing rehearsals. Though Mama had paid a call on Lady Renwick, she left Renwick House well before Antonio and Gianni arrived. Every day it became more difficult to squeeze out the time to practice singing with Caroline. But Susan persisted, both to keep her promise and to have time with Gianni, who almost always was able to spend part of his afternoon at the lesson.

He had not spoken again about taking her to Italy. She still did not know if the invitation was genuine. She only knew that someday she wanted to stand in the places in the pictures of Siena. And she wanted Gianni beside her.

Susan replaced the print on the wall and donned her warmest pelisse. Since Mama never left the house except in the carriage, Susan and Peg had to walk to Renwick House most days.

When she hurried into the music room, she was glad she had worn an extra pair of stockings. Gianni held several pairs of skates.

Caroline was already in place beside the pianoforte. "Come, Susan. We are going to run through our songs quickly. Once Mama leaves for the mantua maker, we are going to the river to skate and see the Frost Fair."

Gianni packed the skates into a large carpetbag. "They say the ice will go out in a few days when the high tides come. If we are to enjoy the celebrations, we must go today."

"Then let us start." To Susan, the plan was perfect. She followed the newspaper's daily reports on the growth of the attractions on the frozen Thames and longed to see the spectacle. The very fact her parents would disapprove made the adventure even more appealing.

An hour later, as they neared the river, they could see the fluttering flags and bright tents and hear the music and laughter. The streets grew crowded with spectators, peddlers, jugglers, and clowns. Once on the ice, they found benches on which to sit while strapping on their skates.

"I have no idea how to get these contraptions on," Antonio said. "I am from warm and sunny Roma. How would I know about these?"

Gianni buckled his skates and reached over to assist Tonio. "Do you know how to skate, *bella mia?*"

"I learned when I was little," Susan said. "We skated when we went to Papa's mother's house in Northumbria."

"Umbria!" Antonio exclaimed. "That is *Italia,* not England."

"No, no. It is an entirely different place, far north of here, sometimes cold and rocky and forbidding. There the pond freezes solid from December to March."

"Ah." Tonio moved his feet cautiously, reaching to hold on to Caroline.

Susan was surprised she remembered so quickly how to move on the skates and was even more surprised at Gianni's skill.

"Do not forget, *cara mia,* I have lived in England for many years. I have not been to Northumbria, but I spent many Christmastides in Yorkshire."

A small orchestra played lively tunes at the edge of the circle that had been scraped and swept for skaters. Susan grasped Gianni's hands and glided beside him around the rim of the plot, around and around, weaving in and out among the other skaters. The air, instead of feeling cold and clammy, now felt crisp and invigorating. Perhaps, she thought, it was the exertion. Not to mention the feel of Gianni's shoulder touching hers and the contact of his hands, even through several layers of wool.

She imagined her cheeks were as cherry red as his were, her eyes as bright, though not so dark. If only she could drive away the dark thoughts that in just a week the St. Valentine's Ball would be over. She would have no rehearsals to take her away from her sisters, no excuses to meet with Gianni.

Perhaps later in the Season, she could again engage him to give her lessons in speaking Italian. Mama might be busy enough with Dianthe and Theodosia that Susan could escape from time to time.

Gianni squeezed her hand and grinned down at her. "Look at Tonio. He has made it twice around the circle."

"I think poor Lady Caroline is holding him up."

Just as she spoke, Tonio lost his balance and was suddenly sliding across the ice on his seat.

Laughing, they skated to him and hauled him to his feet.

"This is enough torture for poor Antonio," he said. "Now I get these awful contraptions off and find the wine merchant."

Gianni cuffed him playfully. "Nothing but frozen lemonade for you, *amico mio!* Your legs are already wobbling."

As they packed their skates, a short man in a red stocking cap grabbed at Gianni's coat.

"Prego, Signor DiFerrante . . ."

Gianni patted Susan's hand. "Excuse me. This will take just a moment." He walked a few feet away, where Gianni bent his head low, his ear almost at the mouth of the other man.

Susan watched the two. These frequent exchanges mystified her. Almost everywhere Gianni went people seemed to need his attention, and their information was treated as though it was secret.

She looked away and caught a glimpse of Caroline gazing at Tonio with eyes full of adoration. Clearly, Caro's feelings transcended anything so mundane as a frigid day. Again, Susan wondered if Lady Renwick was not risking an awful scandal.

Suddenly the day seemed cold, gray, and the chill penetrating. The future looked as bleak as the cloudy sky. What would happen to Caroline and Antonio once the great performance was over next week? How would Susan continue her Italian lessons?

She would have to devise a ruse of some kind. Perhaps Gianni would assist her, since she was certain he needed the money she paid. He received nothing from Lady Renwick, despite his attendance at the singing practice, nor had he shown any sign of other employment. Which again brought up the continuing mystery of just who he was—and what he was doing teaching Italian conversation to a person like herself.

Before she could sink too far into the gloom, Gianni was back at her side, and his grin wiped away her dubious thoughts for the moment.

After munching lovely hunks of cake frosted in white as if they were part of the river's ice, the four of them stood near a huge fire, close enough to feel its warmth penetrate their coats.

For the rest of the afternoon, Susan felt she was in a special kind of paradise. Everywhere she looked, there was a new stall with tempting wares, a performer surrounded by a jolly audience, food vendors of succulent chicken and lamb, fragrant gingerbread, steaming hot chestnuts. The crowd of people ate, ogled, cheered, and danced to the music of a dozen ensembles. At one point,

Gianni swept her into his arms and whirled her around to a boisterous folk tune until she was dizzy.

Scattered over the ice were huge bonfires surrounded by people reaching out to warm their fingers. Everyone talked of nothing but the extraordinary cold and how many times the river had frozen over. Some said in the time of Elizabeth, Charles the Second was said to have hunted fox on the surface of the Thames. Others were certain Cromwell had ordered the river to freeze, and it had obeyed to keep itself out of the stocks. One old man said it had happened last in his youth.

It was growing dark by the time Susan collected Peg at Renwick House and went home. Just before they turned into Brook Street, Gianni stopped and took Susan's hand.

"Bella mia, I shall never forget this afternoon."

Her eyes filled with tears. "Nor shall I, Gianni. Thank you for taking me."

He reached up and, with his forefinger, wiped a tear from her cheek and pressed its moisture to his lips. *"Grazie,* Susanna *mia. Addio."*

Almost blinded by her fog of tears, Susan walked to the corner, then turned and waved. He was standing in the darkening cold, smiling.

Peg took Susan's arm. "Come, miss. Your mama will be worried."

Susan lifted her hand once more, but she could not see Gianni for weeping.

"I find it much easier to discuss the dreadful cold when I am sitting here sweating." The Duke of Bainbridge adjusted the towel wrapped around his waist and leaned back against the tile of the steam bath.

Gianni wiped the sheen of perspiration from his forehead and followed his half brother's example, stretching his legs out before him. "What news I have from the Continent is all bad. I hope to hear more favorable reports from you."

"Humph! If you can call wild rumors of Napoleon's abdication or his assassination favorable. None of it is true. Reliable information is scarce."

Gianni shrugged. "You can consider what my cousin has written to be reliable, sadly so. Nothing coming out of Italy is encouraging to those of us who hoped for progress toward unifying the peninsula. My cousin holds out no hope whatsoever for putting together a provisional government. He and his compatriots are embroiled in arguments with other secret societies. They cannot agree on leadership. They hate Murat."

"I am not surprised. He has changed sides so many times, no one knows where he stands. And his wife is Napoleon's sister, though I have heard she despises her brother."

Gianni watched the moisture drip from the ceiling. He felt every one of his eight years collecting information on Italian affairs had been wasted. "This is a great disappointment to me. I hate admitting more years under foreign control are needed to coalesce all the factions throughout the peninsula. All my sources come to the same conclusion, though few admit it. No one favors bringing back the Austrians, but I do not see what alternative the allied leadership could find."

"I am not surprised," the duke said. "To be honest, I considered it unlikely the Italians could unite under one leader. We will, of course, not stand in their way if they can do so. But I agree with your assessment. Unity is unlikely. I believe many in our government are ready to encourage Metternich."

Gianni wondered if this was how a soldier felt after his regiment had been defeated in battle. When the generals surrendered, could it be any worse? "That thought is more dismal than I could have imagined."

The duke's face was flushed to a bright pink. "I believe, John, you have done as much as you can. If you want to make your way to Tuscany this summer, I have no objection. And I welcome you back to London society as Lord John Stansberry, if you wish to exchange your present rooms for a more comfortable apartment here in Bainbridge House."

"Thank you for your generosity. And thank you for supporting us, especially when you had to oppose some of your best friends."

"You are the one who gave up your way of life. For me, the sacrifice was minimal."

Gianni shook his head. "I know what you stood for. And I appreciate your efforts. Some day I believe the old city states and the regions of Italy will come together. I must learn patience, I suppose."

"Indeed, one must view these things philosophically."

Gianni breathed deeply, filling his lungs with the warm, moist air. "As for resuming my former life, I may do just that."

"I am glad to hear it."

Saying these things out loud gave them an entirely new reality, Gianni thought. "I have met a young lady who has captured a place in my heart. But I do not know quite how I am to metamorphosize from Gianni, the poor Tuscan exile, into Lord John, brother of His Grace the Duke of Bainbridge. She may not take my masquerade kindly."

"If she loves you, she will become accustomed to the idea I predict. Do I know her family?"

"Probably. She is the daughter of Baron Halford, and granddaughter of the late fifth Earl of Traisdel."

"I am acquainted with Halford, and I knew Traisdel in the old days. Sounds like an entirely suitable match for you."

"She sees me as Gianni, who gives lessons in *conversatione Italiano*. I have reason to believe she might regret the, shall we say, familiarity in which we have engaged. She would not have been quite so free if she knew she was dealing with one of her own class."

The duke glowered at his half brother. "Devil take it, John, do not tell me you have compromised the young lady!"

"Of course not. I have been all that is proper. But she calls me Gianni, shares her thoughts about her sisters, went skating with me on the Thames—all sorts of intimacies in which she would never indulge with a gentleman of rank. The dictates of society prevent most couples from experiencing the very things that brought us close in heart and mind."

The duke settled back into a more complacent posture. "Ah, you are indeed a rebel at heart, John. You would overhaul the entire marriage mart, I take it?"

"Indeed I would."

"After our rubdowns, I shall I offer you a cognac and wish you happy. What disappointments you experience in regard to Italy should be well overridden by your success in your personal life."

Gianni smiled. "That is so. Assuming the lady does not have me ejected bodily from her presence when I tell her the truth!"

While Caro and Tonio sang love duets on the other side of the music room in Renwick House, Gianni read a love poem to Susan. She listened to his sweet voice through a haze of pain.

Today was their last afternoon together.

Tomorrow was St. Valentine's Day, the date of the Renwick's ball. She and Lady Caroline would sing, the culmination of their weeks of practice under the direction of Maestro Antonio. If Lady Renwick had her way, Caro would be quite occupied in the next few days accepting flowers and notes, calls and invitations from numerous gentlemen for carriage rides in the park. Lady Renwick would not expect her daughter to continue with music lessons once her singing brought her to the attention of the sort of young men she wished to have as candidates to be her daughter's husband.

"Capisce? Do you understand?" Gianni spoke softly.

"I am sorry, Gianni. I did not catch a word. I was listening, but my head is empty today."

"The poet would be disappointed. He intended the music of the voice to be more appealing. You are supposed to fall into the arms of the lover who recites these words to you."

Susan's eyes widened in surprise. He moved in closer to her and put an arm around her shoulder.

"Carissima mia, sono sopraffare, I am overcome, my darling."

"Is that part of the poem?"

"No, Susanna. I must confess to you now."

"Confess?" She gave a fearful shiver.

He glanced over to ensure Antonio and Caro were paying attention only to one another. "I must tell you the whole story now, my story. Everything I have told you about my family is true. My mother was born in Tuscany and my father was English. He was much older than she and already had a large family here in England. After his first wife died, he went to Firenze and lived there for a while. Eventually he met my mother and married her. She died when I was a mere child."

"So you have said." Susan could not see what point he was trying to make. But she was content to listen to him.

"All of that is true, but what I did not tell you is that my father was the Duke of Bainbridge. My half brother Richard is the duke now, and it is to his house I took you to see the pictures."

She drew away from him and looked up in shock. "What? Does he not acknowledge you? Why do you live like a poor exile?"

"Richard, His Grace, is a close friend and adviser of government ministers. Of course he acknowledges me. To him, I am Lord John Stansberry. I see him nearly every week, and I will soon move back into Bainbridge House, where I have lived on and off all my life."

"Lord John Stansberry? You?" Susan's heart pounded as though she had been running for hours. She snapped her mouth shut, aware she had been gaping in open-jawed incredulity.

"Yes, *cara mia*. That is my name. But my name is also Gianni DiFerrante, the name of my mother's family. You see, this part is truly a secret. And you must never tell a soul."

"I will not."

His voice was barely more than a whisper. "Not even Antonio knows my story. I have been living in the Italian exile community, trying to gather information for His Majesty's government on the activities of various groups in Italia, groups engaged in resistance to local governments installed by Napoleon, groups favoring the unity of all Italian regions, groups in outright rebellion."

"You live a double life?"

"Not exactly. I live among the Italian community. I befriend recent arrivals and listen to their conversations. I hear their news from home. I ask a few questions. I report to my brother or to a contact in the Foreign Office.

Sometimes I write broadsheets to be distributed in Italy to encourage the resistance."

"Gianni, that means you are truly fighting for England, just as much as if you were marching with Lord Wellington."

"Ah, *carissima mia,* if only it were so. Richard is probably the only man in England who would agree with you. I am not sure my information really did much good."

"Gianni, I think you are a hero." She leaned toward him, slipped her arms around his neck, and kissed him on the cheek. "I knew there was more to you than the story you told."

"And what did you think the 'more' was?"

She nuzzled his cheek and kissed his earlobe. "Oh, you will laugh at me. I worried so. At first I though you might be married. You were always whispering to people. At the opera. On the ice. Then I was afraid you were arranging things."

"Aha," Gianni laughed. "You thought I was a procurer, finding young ladies for the pleasure of gentlemen? For shame, *cara mia,* to think I would stoop so low. And what would a fine young lady like you know of such things anyway?"

"That is the problem. I know nothing of such things. So my imagination ran away with me."

As one, they looked across the room and saw Caro and Tonio leaning over a stack of music, with eyes only for each other.

Gianni tipped up her chin and brushed his lips across hers. "Come with me to Italia, Susanna *mia,* come with me to Tuscany, to Siena and Firenze. I will show you everything, and together we will share the light, the wines, the beauties of the countryside. Every day we will visit quaint villages and magnificent *palazzos,* ancient churches, and superb gardens. We will share everything. I will braid flowers in your hair and you will feed me grapes."

"Gianni, are you reading poetry or just talking to me?"

He laughed and drew her into his arms more tightly. "Ah, my Susanna, I speak to you from my heart, right now. Say you will come with me."

"I want to come with you. I want to very much."

Six

Susan quietly crept down to the breakfast room early on the morning of St. Valentine's Day and poured herself a cup of chocolate. No one else would be up yet. Tonight's ball would last until the wee hours of tomorrow morning. Her sisters, Mamma, Papa, and the dowager would be in bed for hours.

Susan did not plan to stay late tonight. She would slip away after she and Caro sang, before the dancing got under way.

She would be much happier at home, dreaming of herself and Gianni on their travels through Italy. If any of the gentlemen at the ball enjoyed her duets, let them pay their respects to Caro. Susan could not imagine flirting with anyone who attended tonight.

After all, she had Gianni. Or should she be calling him Lord John now? Last night her head had been too crowded with dreams of the two of them together in Siena to have room to think of his double life. She dropped off to sleep before she absorbed the implications of the truth about his subterfuge.

"Good morning, Susan." Theodosia took a seat at the breakfast table.

"What are you doing up so early? You should be sleeping at least until noon."

"I am much too nervous. Dianthe is awake too. Both

of us are too excited to sleep. Do you think anyone will ask me to dance with him? Now that the time is near, I declare my knees are already shaking."

Susan smiled at her younger sister. Theodosia's delicate beauty was likely to bring her many partners, and probably a host of suitors. Even several offers of marriage. And the same would be true of Dianthe. Both were lovely, fresh and innocent, yet accomplished enough to attract the approbation of the *ton*'s most exacting and influential leaders.

Until Susan created a scandal by running off with the brother of the Duke of Bainbridge. The thought hit her like a Thames ice floe crashing into a bridge support. If she became the object of society's gossip, the disgrace would ruin Theodosia's season. And Dianthe's. Mama would be forced to take them home, their reputations stained by their sister's indiscretions.

Though Theodosia continued to chatter, Susan felt drawn into another world, empty, alone, and flustered. If she followed her dreams, followed her heart, she would be spoiling everything for her sisters.

Dianthe burst into the room with a shriek of excitement. "Susan! You have received a St. Valentine greeting." She waved a square of folded vellum. "Who is it from? You must open it and tell us immediately."

Susan broke the seal. About ten lines of Italian verse filled the page under the heading, "A Valentine Poem."

"Who is it from?" Dianthe tried to peer over her shoulder to look for a signature.

Before her eyes misted over, Susan made out the symbol at the end of the poem. It was the simple shape of a heart.

She left her sisters gaping at her in openmouthed surprise as she raced from the room in a deluge of tears.

* * *

Peg stood back from Susan's chair and admired her work.

"You look beautiful, Miss Susan. I think a simple style is most becomin.'"

"Thank you, Peg. It is just fine." Susan hardly peeked at the mirror. She did not care if her hair looked as if a windmill arranged it. She did not care if her dress flattered her figure or made her look like a stump. She did not care if her gloves were smudged, her earrings mismatched, or her stockings torn.

For the most part, she felt numb, almost paralyzed with disappointment and grief. The St. Valentine's Day poem from Gianni lay on her dressing table, mostly untranslated. She had been unable to concentrate all day. A few phrases she recognized, but whenever she looked at it, she started to cry. Through her tears, she had trouble deciphering its meaning. Phrases such as "tyrannous love" and "beautiful caresses" were clear, but the context eluded her understanding.

The Valentine poem represented all she ardently desired but could not have. She prided herself on—had even bragged to Gianni—about her unconventionality, her independence, her disdain for society's rules. But now, though she still held these views for herself, she knew she could not act upon them. Her concern for her sisters must prevail. Fairness was more important than indulging her opinions and flaunting society's dictates.

No matter how much she wanted to throw herself into Gianni's plan to go to Italy, she could not bring herself to endanger her sisters' futures. There were limits to the selfish things she would do. Perhaps it was fortunate she could not read the words in the valentine.

If she never saw Gianni again, it would be for the

best. She could send him a letter at the duke's house and explain her decision. She would ask him not to contact her again. A meeting would be too painful, not to mention tempting.

Later, after she finished singing, she hoped she could come directly home. In case she could not escape promptly, she stuffed the valentine into her reticule. She would find herself a secluded corner of Renwick House if it meant sitting in the pantry. There she could try again to read it. Or, as she had done all afternoon, she could simply stare at the page, trace the letters with her finger, and think of how he had written it.

"Are you ready, Susan?" Lady Serena swept into the bedchamber in a cloud of rosy scent.

"Yes, I am."

"I hope your singing goes well for you this evening, my dear. Your sisters tell me you received a St. Valentine's Day greeting. Will the young man who sent it be at the Renwick's ball tonight?"

Susan shook her head. "I do not think so."

"That is quite a pity. But there may be some gentlemen new to the Season. Be sure to keep smiling."

"Yes. I will." At the moment, Susan felt more like indulging in a good cry.

Lady Serena rearranged a lock of Susan's hair. "I hope this evening is successful for both you and Lady Caroline. I cannot imagine how Elaine concocted such a harebrained scheme."

"To have Caro sing?"

"The part about that Italian fellow she hired. Did you not know Caro's mother intended for her to fall in love with him?"

"With Maestro Antonio?"

"Her voice teacher, whatever his name is. Elaine told me she thought Caroline would be more attractive to other men if 'Caro wore the radiance of love,' I believe the phrase was."

Susan shook her head in amazement. "I did not know . . ."

"I told Elaine I thought it was a miracle Caro had not run off to Gretna Green with the fellow already. Did she fall in love with him?"

Susan pressed her fingertips to her temples. She hated telling these fibs, but what choice did she have? "I never noticed."

"Then perhaps she was immune to his foreign charms. Or perhaps it was your presence that prevented the disaster. Come along, dear. It is time to depart."

When the Halford carriage reached Renwick House that evening, Susan almost gasped at the blaze of flame that lit its façade. Inside, the rooms seemed lit by a million candles. Papa squeezed Susan's hand and gave her a fond smile.

"Sing well, my dear."

Susan nodded and watched her family join the crowd on the staircase. As planned, she entered the back hall and went up the servants' stairs. Antonio whispered into Caro's ear, whether endearments or encouragement, Susan could not hear.

"Are you ready?" Caro asked.

Susan shrugged. "Whenever you are."

For a few minutes, time seemed suspended as they waited for the audience on the other side of the door to quiet and for Caro's father to make the introductions.

At last they walked into the music room and took their familiar places around the pianoforte.

Susan's numbness seemed to enhance rather than spoil her singing with Lady Caroline. The nervous stomach and shaking hands she expected never materialized. Instead Susan pasted an artificial smile on her face and let the long hours of practice guide her voice. Even through her haze, she knew Caro was in fine form this evening.

To Susan, it seemed their songs were finished almost before they began. Applause broke into her dreamy state and she curtsied to the accolades of the audience. A group of people crowded around Lady Caroline, and Susan got just a quick glimpse of the glowing smile on Lady Renwick's face.

Gradually, Susan backed away from the eager chatter surrounding her. She knew her smile remained in place because her facial muscles seemed tightly frozen. No one seemed to notice as she slipped behind two men in evening finery, then stepped in between some groups of people and eventually into the foyer.

Its only other occupant was Antonio, his music under his arm. "Miss Susan, you were verra' fine tonight. I am sorry Gianni could not hear."

"Yes. A pity. Are you staying for the dancing?"

He gave a regretful laugh. "No, I leave now."

"But—"

"It's-a what I expect. *Finito.* My job is over. From this night I get more jobs helping more young ladies. More work, more money."

"But you and Caro are . . . ah, such good friends."

"Si. L'amici. Now she finds a young man her mama likes."

"But I know Caro feels so much for you. She will never forget you."

Antonio's smile, as always, was broad and earnest. "No, she never forgets me. When she is upset, angry with her husband some-a day, she thinks of Antonio and she is happy again, *capisce?"*

Susan felt a lump in her throat. "Yes, I think I understand you."

"Arrivederci, Signorina Susan." Antonio took her hand and raised it to his lips, bowed, and headed for the stairs. Without turning back, he went down to make his departure.

Susan wiped away a tear. So this was how Caro's little adventure ended, with a crowd of eligible gentlemen surrounding her but with her maestro in both music and love leaving her life forever. Susan felt as bleak as the frozen wastes of the February countryside.

She would probably never see Gianni again, either. As Antonio predicted for Caro, Susan would never forget Gianni DiFerrante. Someday, when she achieved her dream of visiting Italy, she would go to Siena and haunt the Campo, yearning for him to be there, too. But by then, he would probably be in love with someone else or even married.

Unconsciously she fingered the reticule holding his poem. She had better find Mama and see if she could order the carriage to take her home. The rest of this evening belonged to Caro and her swains, to Dianthe and Theodosia, to the beginning of another London Season. All she wanted for herself was to be in her own bedchamber with her Italian books, her Italian prints, and her overflowing imagination.

People spilled into the foyer where she stood, several greeting her and complimenting her on her singing. Susan thanked them for their good wishes and headed back into the music room to find her mama and sisters.

Unexpectedly, to her total shock, she saw Gianni and almost cried out in surprise.

He stood not far away in a group of young men around Caroline, resplendent in black formal evening clothes. Several people bumped against her as Susan stood rooted to the floor, unable to move, panting as if she had been running hard.

She knew she was staring, but could not stop herself. His smile was as dazzling as ever. The little curl she loved to brush back had drooped over his forehead. He was so much the quintessence of all she wanted she could not look away.

As she watched, Gianni offered his arm to Caroline and they moved in her direction, accompanied by a clutch of gentlemen. She stood motionless, entirely at a loss for words.

When Gianni passed her, Susan was sure he looked right through her, not seeing her at all.

She felt as though someone slammed her in the stomach, knocking the air from her lungs and leaving her limply struggling for breath. Susan was staring not at Gianni, but at Lord John Stansberry, and he had not so much as a flicker of an eyebrow for her.

"At last I found you," her mother said, putting her arm around Susan's shoulders. "You were excellent, my dear."

"I am proud of you, Susan." Lord Halford kissed her cheek.

"You did not look frightened in the least." Dianthe grabbed Susan's hand.

"And there were at least a hundred people looking at you." Theodosia shook her head, making her dozens of blond ringlets bounce up and down. "I could never do that."

Like a puppet, Susan was pulled along toward the ballroom. "Mama, I must find the ladies' retiring room." *Anyplace to get away.* "I fear I am getting the headache."

"Do you have a powder to take?"

"Yes," Susan fibbed. Headache powder would have no effect whatsoever on the volcanic emotions she felt now. "I will find you later."

Susan sidestepped the next group of people and

returned to the music room, where the pianoforte stood deserted in front of the ranks of now empty chairs. The little settee where Gianni often sat had been pushed into line with the last row, and she sat down to gather her thoughts.

If only she could go back to her happiness of yesterday, when she was dreaming of travel to Italy with Gianni. Everything that happened since this morning would be wiped away. The nightmare of the last few minutes, seeing Gianni fawning over Lady Caroline, being given the cut direct, all that would not have happened.

She sat alone for a long time. All she could think of was Gianni and his inexplicable snub. Nothing else. When the footmen eventually came to move the chairs away, she had not managed a single rational explanation for his behavior.

She wandered back into the foyer, wondering if she dared get her wrap and just leave, find their carriage, and ask to be taken home immediately. Or she could walk. The ice had mostly thawed; the only loss would be her silken slippers. The way she felt, she would never need them again anyway, for surely this was the very last ball she would ever attend.

"I cannot imagine where she has disappeared." Lady Renwick came out of the ballroom accompanied by Gianni.

Susan froze in place.

"Why here she is! Susan, this gentleman, Lord John Stansberry, is recently returned to town after a long absence. He wishes to be made known to you. Lord John, this is Miss Kimball, my daughter's vocal partner."

Gianni bowed low. By rote, she dipped a little curtsy.

"Miss Kimball, I compliment you on your very fine performance with Lady Caroline."

His voice was familiar, warm. She wanted to weep for loving its tone so much.

Lady Renwick patted Susan's arm. "Now I shall leave you. I have a thousand things to attend to."

Gianni continued. "You must have spent a great deal of time practicing together." He cast a look at Lady Renwick being swallowed up by the crowd in the ballroom. "Susanna *mia,* you have my highest praise. You were wonderful."

"But, Gianni, I mean Lord John . . . you walked right past me."

"We had not been introduced. How could I pretend to know you?"

Susan still felt lost. "You mean Lord John was never introduced to me?"

"Exactly, *cara mia.* What explanation would I have for being acquainted with you if I had been away from England?"

"What did Lady Renwick say when she saw you? And Caro?"

Gianni took her hands in his. "Ah, Susan, if they noticed a resemblance between Lord John Stansberry and Gianni DiFerrante, they never mentioned it."

"You mean they did not know you?"

"People of Society do not look very closely at menials. It never entered Lady Renwick's head that I am also the Gianni who spent so many afternoons in her music room. Nor could such a strange idea have occurred to Lady Caroline, especially when she was so excited after your performance. When they heard the name of Lord John Stansberry, Gianni DiFerrante was far from their thoughts. But you recognized me, *carissima mia.* Come with me into the ballroom."

He led her to the edge of the guests assembled to watch the dancing. "We can join the next set."

Susan gave a little gasp and backed away. Abruptly the sadness of the occasion overwhelmed her and she fought to control her threatening tears. "Oh, no, we cannot. Come back to the foyer, please."

His expression quizzical, he returned with her to the anteroom.

"Gianni, I must explain. I must . . . Oh, I have to tell you I cannot go to Italy."

"What?" He looked stricken, then broke into a smile. "Do not tease, *dolci mia*."

"It would be a terrible scandal. It would ruin my sisters and perhaps kill my mother." Susan let all her fears and doubts tumble out. "I thought I was able to make my own decisions. I thought I could be as unconventional as I wanted to be. But I cannot. I have obligations to my family. When I go to Italy, it will be as I told you when we met, as a companion to a lady or governess to a child."

She searched for a handkerchief, but there had not been room, since the folded-up poem filled her reticule.

He handed her his own handkerchief and kissed the tear that spilled down her cheek. "It is all there in my Valentine poem."

"I could not read it. I knew some of the words but not enough, and the grammar is beyond me." She choked back her weeping and dried her eyes. "Now as Lord John, you cannot tutor me. I will search out a new tutor, then find a position." She tried to smile. "After all, you had excellent suggestions for my advertisement in the *Times*."

A large man of late middle years joined them, putting his arm around Gianni. "Please introduce me to Miss Kimball."

Gianni cast him a fond look. "May I present His Grace, the Duke of Bainbridge, Miss Kimball. Richard, I was just about to tell Susan I would like to announce our betrothal in a few weeks. In fact, I hope to speak to her father here tonight."

Susan wondered if she had strayed into a scene from a drama or one of those silly pantomimes. Nothing made sense to her.

His Grace and his brother continued to talk for a few moments. Susan hoped she was saying the right things and making the correct gestures. She could not stop looking at Gianni, focusing on his shapely lips as he formed the words, though these were in English and not in the Italian she was trying to imitate.

She realized the duke was speaking to her. "You have a lovely voice, Miss Kimball. I look forward to hearing you frequently as a member of my family."

She fought to recover her poise. "Thank you, Your Grace."

The duke bowed again. "John, I shall see you later. Miss Kimball, it has been my pleasure."

Gianni clasped her hand as she curtsied deeply.

The duke disappeared down the stairs.

Gianni grinned. "My brother is the soul of discretion."

"He was indeed kind to me."

"Susan, where is your father? I wish to speak to him as soon as possible."

"My father?"

"Of course, *carissima mia.* I need to see your father to ask for your hand in marriage."

She shook her head in astonishment and took a trembling breath. "Ask for my hand?"

"Well, ask to call upon you. He would no doubt think me a clod if I proposed marriage after one evening's acquaintance. I have an idea. Come with me." He took her hand and led her downstairs to the ground floor, through the entrance hall and into a tiny room. "This is where Antonio and I left our coats."

He shut the door. The only light came through a small window from the flambeaux placed outside. "Let me explain. I spoke with my brother the other day and told him about you. He agrees that my services to His Majesty's government are nearly over. He gave us his blessing, though we will have to wait a few weeks to announce our betrothal. No one will ever know we have known one another for many weeks already."

Susan still did not understand. "Betrothal? But what about going off to Italy?"

"My work here is over. We will make our voyage a wedding trip."

"You say betrothal, wedding. I am confused."

"Did you not read my Valentine capriccio?"

"I could not translate all the words."

"I fear I am a poor poet, but I tried to say everything there. I titled it 'A Valentine Poem,' and know that my feelings are not capricious. My love is anything but a fantasy, *cara mia.*"

Susan felt the melting need begin inside her. Or perhaps the feeling was Peg's fluttering chicks.

Gianni continued. "We could run away to Italy together as lovers if we were Susanna and Gianni. But as Susan and John, we must take the conventional route, be true to our families."

Was she hearing things? Was this an illusion? Or was he truly here, talking to her?

"Susanna *mia,* I promise you when we are married, we will always be Susanna and Gianni to each other. Our lives will be filled with poetry and moments of unexpected joy."

"Gianni? Are you speaking to me or reading a poem?"

He laughed and pulled her into his arms. "I do not wonder that my poem was incomprehensible. All I

know is that we must be together." He kissed her forehead. "Now can we go find your father?"

"He despises balls. He came only to see me sing. If
he is still here, he will be in the card room. But, Gianni,
wait."

"Yes, *carissima mia?*"

"If you are going to ask him if you may court me, do
you not think you should have my permission first?"

He held her close and spoke into her hair. "Do I not
already have your pledge to go to Italy with me?"

"That was Susanna speaking to Gianni."

"Then, my dear Miss Kimball, I humbly beg your
consent to my petition to your father asking to pay my
addresses to you. Is that proper enough for you?"

She drew back to see his face. "It sounds perfectly
appropriate for Lord John Stansberry. I agree."

The laughter in his eyes softened, changing to the
glow of passion. He wrapped his arms tightly around
her. *"Bellissima mia,* have I told you how lovely you
look tonight?

She leaned into him, crushing his cravat, and turned
up her face for his kiss.

But instead of touching his mouth to hers, his lips
were at her ear, whispering softly. *"Te amo, carissima
mia. Te amo."*

THE UGLY DUCKLING'S VALENTINE

Julia Parks

For Aunt Sister and Uncle J.T.,
with love

"All my sweet children here at my table, and not an ugly one in the bunch," said Lady Sheffield. Her gaze traveled the length of the table, from the first daughter and son-in-law to the next daughter and son-in-law, on to the budding beauty of her twin granddaughters, to her son and his boon companion Lord Kittridge and finally coming to rest on her youngest, Lady Claire.

Lady Claire rolled her eyes and pursed her lips before taking a bite of the trifle before her; in her exasperation, she forgot the cook sometimes added a bit of coconut to her specialty. Grimacing, Claire lifted her napkin to her lips, hoping to dispose of the stringy mess discreetly. Her fatal mistake, however, was looking up and discovering she had an audience—Viscount Kittridge, her brother's devilishly handsome, extremely sophisticated friend. His dancing eyes, as black as coal, were her undoing. She choked, spewing the contents of her mouth across the snowy tablecloth.

"Really, brat," said her older brother, jumping up and pounding her between the shoulders, "Do we have to send you to the nursery with little Henry?"

Twisting away from his vigorous treatment, Claire was still unable to speak and so stuck out her tongue.

The Earl of Sheffield resumed his seat at the head of the table. "Oh, how very refined."

"I must protest, Sheffield, and champion the lady. I mean, of all people, you should know that any action, however, uh, childish, can appear quite charming, if performed with a certain panache. And if I may be so bold, Lady Claire, you stuck out your tongue in the most enchanting manner I have ever witnessed."

"Why, thank you, my lord," she simpered.

"And the trifle decorating the cloth?" asked her brother, his own eyes—often remarked upon for their similarity to the color of the greenest grass—beginning to twinkle.

"A trifling matter," said the viscount, winking at his friend's little sister.

A knife being tapped against a crystal goblet caught their attention. All eyes returned to the matriarch at the end of the long table.

"My dears, as you know, St. Valentine's Day will soon be upon us, and as you also know, we will be here in London this year, since our gentlemen are attending Parliament. I have decided, however, that we must give our usual ball."

"How wonderful, Mother!" said Lady Northam.

"May we watch from the gallery, Papa?" asked Pammy, one of the Northams' twins.

"Now, now, you know I leave all social matters entirely in the hands of your mother."

"May we, Mother?" asked Sophie, her green eyes sparkling like emeralds. "Oh, I wish we were old enough to attend," she added dreamily.

"Pray, do not rush such matters, love. You and Pammy may watch from the gallery, but only until ten o'clock."

"Ten? Oh please, Mama, can we not stay up until midnight?" breathed Pammy.

The parents exchanged glances, and their father said, "Until eleven o'clock, and not a minute later."

"Thank you, Papa! Thank you, Mama!"

"Would you like some help planning the ball?" asked the second eldest daughter, Lady Melton.

"Now, Regina, you mustn't work too hard," said her doting husband, the handsome Lord Melton.

"No, we shan't let her work too hard, Melton," said her sister, Lady Northam.

"Yes, girls, I can certainly use all your help. In the country, it was simple to plan a ball. One didn't have so many choices to make. Here in London, it will be much more difficult."

"I can see this meal is going to degenerate into a strategic planning session," said Robert, the Earl of Sheffield. "Gentlemen, perhaps we should leave the ladies here and go to the drawing room for our port."

"Do not be impertinent, Robert," said his mother. "Certainly you may leave, if you wish, but your sisters and I will be the ones adjourning to the drawing room." The matriarch rose and set sail. "Come along, girls. I have made sure there is paper and ink in the escritoire, Regina, so you will make our lists for us, won't you?"

The purple-gowned Lady Sheffield, who had only recently ended a year of mourning for her late husband, led the procession. Her eldest daughter, Rebecca, followed close on her heels. Then came her second child, Regina, and finally Lady Claire, the youngest daughter of the illustrious Sheffield family. Pammy and Sophie, Rebecca's fourteen-year-old twins, caught up with their grandmother, holding her hands as they chattered happily about the coming ball.

In the drawing room, the twins perched on footstools, eagerly soaking up every detail about the ball to come. Lady Sheffield and Rebecca fired off ideas like volleys of cannons while Regina, who was in a delicate condition, wrote furiously. Hoping to remain obscure, Claire sank onto the small settee by the fire. Extracting her book from behind the pillow where she had hidden it earlier, she immediately lost herself in the rather off-color tale *Tristram Shandy*.

Some time later, Claire started and exclaimed in protest as the book was plucked from her hands. "Robert, pray do not . . ." she began, before the accusation against her brother died on her lips. "Oh! It's you, Kit!" she said, her breath coming out in a rush with the words as her gaze traveled past snug black trousers and snowy cravat, finally taking in the handsome face of her brother's friend.

"Not a very civil greeting for your knight in shining armor," said Viscount Kittridge, sitting down beside her and turning to face her, one arm resting casually on the back of the settee, his fingers teasing her brown curls.

"I'm sorry, Kit. I didn't realize it was you."

"Now I have been insulted," he said softly.

"Hardly. I mistook you for my brother only until I glanced past your . . . that is, when I looked higher than . . . uh, when I saw your face."

He chuckled at her discomfiture, saying softly, "You should blush more often, my dear. It is most becoming."

"Oh, yes," she drawled. "And when I cry, I am like a woodland fawn, with my splotchy face and red eyes."

There was that chuckle again—a low rumble coming from deep inside his broad chest. Oh, if only she could . . .

"I didn't realize fawns had splotchy complexions and bloodshot eyes. Now, if you had said your eyes were wide and deep brown like a fawn's, and your hair, with just the hint of gold, was as soft as a fawn's . . . well, then I might agree with your comparison."

He accompanied this outrageous flattery with a speaking glance, and Claire giggled, relaxing once again in the company of the man who had won her heart when she was but six and he, the impressive age of fourteen. Not that she had ever told him so, and the possibility that he might have guessed . . . Well, through the years, she had learned to hide her feelings.

Still, it was pleasant to be beside one of the most charming and handsome men of the *ton,* and to be able to call him friend.

"I should thank you for rescuing me at the table, Kit."

"No thanks are necessary," he said, pulling a small notebook and pencil from the inner pocket of his elegant coat and studying it earnestly. "Quite the opposite, m'lady. I see I haven't met my quota of rescuing fair damsels for the month of January, and here we are, with only ten days to go."

She giggled, the sound coming quite naturally in this comfortable setting. Her eyes darkened, and her brow furrowed at the thought of the weeks to come. Being thrown into the social whirl, her giggles would be at an end. Instead, any attempt at a flirtatious trill of giggles would doubtless come out in a grating bray. How she dreaded the entire ordeal!

"Why the worried face, CeeCee?" he whispered.

She smiled at him, her eyes filling with sudden tears. Whatever was the matter with her? She never cried! But his use of her childhood nickname had unmanned her— *if such a term might be considered accurate,* came the unspoken thought. This time, however, she only giggled again, giving her brother's friend a watery smile and putting him at his ease once more.

"You know, Claire, if you need anything, anything at all, you've only to ask. I mean, I may not be your real big brother, but I do count myself your unofficial brother."

She patted his arm and nodded. Kit winked at her, and then turned his attention to the book on the seat between them.

"Tristram Shandy," he murmured, eyeing her with raised brows. "Not precisely required reading at the Academy for Proper and Dull Young Ladies.

"It was in the library," she said, not meeting his eyes. "Besides, I have been out of the schoolroom for over two years."

"Ah, yes. Then tell me, Grandmother, what do you think about the winding of the clock metaphor?"

The question was designed to make her blush again, but she refused to give Kit the satisfaction. She met his eyes boldly and said, "A suitable metaphor, given the characters Mr. Stearne has painted."

He chuckled and shook his head. "Most outrageous, my dear, and most unsuitable. If you must read such a work, you must learn to look suitably puzzled when a gentleman questions you over the more lusty portions of the book."

Claire smiled sweetly, opening her dark eyes wide. "And so I shall, my lord, when a *gentleman* asks me."

"Touché," he said, his deep laugh breaking forth again.

"I suppose you are like Rebecca and want me to read suitably dull novels like Richardson's *Pamela,* which I take leave to inform you is an utterly frightful bore. And if I ever behave in such a nonsensical fashion, I pray Robert will have me shut away!"

"No, no, I shan't suggest you read that. Instead, I shall lend you my copy of *Shamela.* I think you will enjoy its irony."

"Shamela?" she asked.

"Yes, written not long after *Pamela* as a parody—quite wicked, so you should enjoy it enormously. But tell me, are you not swooning over the new authoress Miss Austen?"

"I have avoided her novels."

"And why would you do that? Everyone who has read her work loves it, especially the ladies."

"It sounds petty to admit it, but the fact that Rebecca and Regina simply adore her work is the reason I choose not to read it."

"You have a very low opinion of your older sisters," said Kit with a frown.

"No, no, they are wonderful, but they have become terribly staid in the past five or six years."

"Staid? Lady Northam and Lady Melton, two of the leading hostesses of the *ton?*"

"Oh, very well. They are witty, intelligent, and even a bit forward thinking in their views, but they are hardly dashing—beautiful, of course, but not dashing. And I . . . I would love to cut a dash this Season," she added wistfully.

"And so you shall, my dear child. London is waiting on pins and needles for the next Sheffield sister to arrive," said Kit, lifting her hand and kissing her fingertips.

Claire rolled her eyes and would have told him to put a sock in it, but her attention was diverted.

"Claire darling, Mother has had the most wonderful idea," said the eldest Sheffield sister, Lady Northam, her commanding voice carrying throughout the room. "I will give a small card party next week to introduce you to a few of our close friends. Then a day or two later, Regina will host an intimate dinner and an evening at the theater. That way you will have some acquaintances as the other invitations come in. By the time

Mother's grand St. Valentine's Day ball arrives, you will have a host of suitors."

"Oh fudge," muttered Claire as she leaned forward, giving everyone a tight little smile.

"Now, Claire, do not be like that," said her mother. "You will enjoy yourself excessively once the fun begins."

"Yes, Mother," she said obediently.

"You'll see, m' dear. By the night of our ball, your heart will be filled with cards and posies and all manner of little trinkets from your admirers," said Regina, Lady Melton.

Claire mustered up a brighter smile for her; how could she not? Regina was one of those souls who saw the very best in everyone she met, and she had never uttered a word against anyone.

"You're very sweet, Regina," she said.

"Not at all, I . . . Oh, Mother, you did remember to bring the boxes, didn't you?"

Lady Sheffield laughed and nodded. "Of course I did. It would not be St. Valentine's Day without our heart-shaped boxes."

The entire room breathed a sigh of relief.

"I remember the first time, after I had had the boxes made. Claire, you were not a year old, so you wouldn't remember. Everyone was so concerned, frightened that the French might raise an army against us. And then your father decided he should rejoin his regiment, though I could not see what good a man of forty could do to keep Napoleon in his place. I was so angry with him for leaving."

"And then the presents started to arrive," said Sophie, gazing up at her grandmother, her green eyes glowing with interest.

"Yes, a new package every day from the first day of

February until St. Valentine's Day, when your grandfather returned to us."

"So you asked the gardener, Mr. Potter, for a wooden box to place the trinkets in," said Pammy.

"Yes, and it was beautiful, heart-shaped, with a lid. But by the time he had finished carving it, all the bonbons were eaten and the trinkets put away, so I had him carve *Rebecca* on the lid of that box and asked him to make others for each of you. And so he has. Why, we have twelve boxes now," said Lady Sheffield, beaming at each of them in turn. "That reminds me, I must see to it that I send William and Nicholas their packages at school this year. Do not let me forget, Claire."

"I'll remind you, Mother, but I think you have miscounted."

"Miscounted? I don't think so. All I need do is count heads in this room. There are nine of you, including our Kit, plus the boys at school and little Henry asleep upstairs. That makes twelve boxes."

"Yes, but we decided twelve was not a very convenient number, Mother," said her son, striding across the room to pull back the curtains. When he turned, he held a large, heart-shaped box, carved in wood, with the name *Mother* etched into the top.

Lady Sheffield gasped, and tears sprang to her eyes.

"Oh, how wonderful!" she exclaimed, accepting the box while her family leaned in for a closer look. "But it's too big, much larger than the others."

"We decided it would need to be, with all of us contributing to it each day."

"Oh, you are all so . . . oh . . ." Lady Sheffield accepted her son-in-law's handkerchief and wiped her eyes.

"Where will you put the boxes this year, Grandmother?" asked Pammy.

"On the trestle table in the hall. That way, you may visit every day and find your treats as you enter the house."

"I remember when I met Andrew," said Regina, Lady Melton. "I could have filled all our boxes."

"You cannot blame me. I had to do something to gain your attention," said Lord Melton, sitting on the arm of his wife's chair and smiling down at her.

"I daresay Claire only wanted you to have the big box, Mother, to hold all the trinkets she will be receiving when all the young men meet her."

"That is not true, Robert," said Claire. She knew he was only teasing, but she had no illusions about taking London society by storm. All she really hoped for was to find one person who would hold her in esteem.

"Well, it is true, little sister. Once those fellows get a look at you and have a word or two with you . . . Well, I can tell you, my job as your guardian is going to be very tricky indeed," said her brother, causing Claire's blush to deepen.

She looked from his handsome face, with the signature auburn hair and green eyes, to each member of her family. Even her two brothers-in-law were handsome men.

"If you'll excuse me, Mother, I have the headache," she said, rising suddenly and making her way to the door without waiting for any more bracing speeches.

Once free of the drawing room, Claire took flight, speeding across the narrow hall of the elegant town house and up the stairs to safety. She skidded to a halt at the top, whirling around to face her pursuer.

"Claire, what's the matter with you?" said Robert, clutching her arm, his eyes filled with concern instead of a rebuke.

She could take his teasing or temper, but this kindness brought tears to her eyes. Stamping her small foot, Claire dashed them away.

"Robert, I'm sorry. I just don't understand why you and Mother and everyone else refuses to see what's in front of your eyes. I am not Regina or Rebecca, with their auburn hair and beautiful green eyes. I am plain, brown-eyed, brown-haired—and short, too."

"I don't see that that . . ."

"No, you don't, and neither do they, and I love you all for it, but I am not going to *take,* and everyone's insistence that I will have suitors falling at my feet is just ridiculous! If there is one thing I have learned in all my reading, it is that fairy tales do not come true, and while my dowry will lend me a modicum of attractiveness, I will never be the belle of our sacred St. Valentine's Day ball!"

"Claire!" called her brother as she turned on her heel and sped out of sight.

"Let her go, Robert," said his friend, who had waited a few steps below during Claire's heart-wrenchingly blunt declaration.

The Earl of Sheffield turned, shaking his head.

"Mother is not going to like this," he said.

"Well, old boy, perhaps she needn't know." In response to his friend's puzzled frown, Kit grinned and said, "All little Claire needs is a bit of confidence. I vow, the girl is every bit as attractive as her older sisters. She may not have their height, but she has grace and charm, a delightful laugh, and enough wit and conversation to please any discerning man throughout a lifetime. What she doesn't have is confidence."

"And what can you or I do to give her that confidence?" asked Robert.

"Come with me to the study," said the viscount, his black eyes beginning to sparkle. He led his friend down the stairs and toward the back of the house, his steps as sure as any family member's might be. Viscount Kittridge, who had been orphaned at eight and then raised by solicitors and servants, felt more at home among the Sheffield family than anywhere else in the world. Indeed, Robert was more like a brother to him than a mere friend, and Lady Sheffield had welcomed him as one of her own since his first visit home with Robert at the age of nine.

Robert watched in growing amusement as his friend settled himself behind the massive desk that had once belonged to his father. Kit repaired the point on the pen and dipped it in the ink, pausing only a moment before beginning to write. With a flourish, he handed the paper to Robert.

"What do you think?"

"Oh, it's fine. I like the bit about not wanting to frighten her with his ardor, though I'm certain Claire will think it's naught but rubbish. You had best rewrite the thing, disguising your handwriting, or she will see through it in a heartbeat. Wait, look through that bottom drawer and find some older paper. She's not a fool, you know. She comes in here all the time to read. If she notices the writing paper from her love letter is the same as this, she'll tumble to our little game in a flash."

"Right you are," said Kit, rummaging through the drawer his friend had indicated. "What's this?"

He pulled out an old card, the ink of the message smeared and faded, but the cover was still in good shape, and the painted pink roses were quite pretty. The edges had been trimmed in lace.

"Must be one of Regina's or Rebecca's old admirers. Let's use the cover," said the earl.

"No, it has to be older than that," said Kit, carefully

separating the painted cover from the sentimental verse. "I wager it was one of your mother's admirers."

"Well, she'll never miss it, not after all these years. The verse isn't bad. Add this bit about counting the hours."

On the back of the watercolor roses, Kit copied his message again, adding the lines from the old card and disguising his writing. He signed it simply, *An Admirer.*

"There. Now I'll save this until after Rebecca's card party. Then I will slip it into Claire's heart-shaped box, and everyone, including Claire, will assume it is from someone she has met there. And then little Claire will begin to see that she can be the belle of the ball."

Claire's luxurious brown hair was piled on top of her head; it sparkled with tiny paste jewels that her maid Nellie had painstakingly threaded in and out. Her gown was a pale yellow silk, her mother judging that her half a Season two years before had elevated her from the ranks of the schoolgirls just making their debuts. A good thing, too, as Lady Sheffield told her two older daughters, because an insipid white muslin would wash out Claire's complexion, leaving her looking hollow-eyed. The subtle yellow, however, with its simple, flowing lines, was perfect.

Indeed, thought Claire as she looked at the results of an hour's preparation, her appearance was quite pass-able. Oh, she wasn't worthy of the Sheffield name. Her sisters and even her mother would always outshine her perhaps, but tonight she was not an antidote.

"Thank you, Nellie. You have outdone yourself tonight. I look fine enough to attend one of the queen's drawing rooms."

"You look beautiful," breathed the older woman,

smiling fondly at her young mistress. She had had the dressing of both Rebecca and Regina, and had even helped Lady Sheffield through her first Season more than thirty years ago. "You will take London by storm, child, just like your dear mama and sisters did."

"You are quite a dear to think so, but now I must put it to the test."

Claire squared her shoulders and picked up her reticule. Her brother was calling on them to escort them to Rebecca's elegant town house. She wished Kit would come, too, but somehow she could not imagine him at an insipid card party, playing silver loo.

Pausing at the top of the stairs, she shut her eyes and took a deep breath. There was no turning back now. If she were lucky, she would meet some plain, shy young man who would appreciate her intelligence, and not worry about her lack of beauty. If she were very lucky, he would marry her quickly and take her back to the country to become his dull wife without her having to endure the coming Season.

"Are you just going to stand there like a looby all night?" demanded her brother from the foot of the stairs.

Claire opened her eyes and her mouth, prepared to give him the setdown he so richly deserved for teasing her on this night. Instead, her breath caught in her throat.

There was Kit, smiling up at her, his black eyes flashing with gold in the light of the chandelier hanging above the entrance hall. His dress was always impeccable, but tonight he appeared more handsome than ever, from his snowy cravat with its winking onyx pin, to his knit pantaloons and fitted black coat.

"Ignore this impatient nodcock, Claire," he said, taking the steps two at a time until he attained the landing, swept her an elegant bow, and offered her his arm. "You look positively ravishing tonight, my dear."

"So do you, Kit," she managed, causing him to chuckle. "I didn't know you were coming tonight."

"What, miss your bow into Society? I think not. Besides, your mother asked me particularly. Shall we?"

Well, that explained it, thought Claire. Everyone jumped to do her sweet mother's bidding.

With her free hand, Claire held her skirts out of the way and willed herself not to tumble head over heels down the steps. She heaved a sigh of relief when they reached the marble hall below.

"Quite fetching," said her brother, giving her appearance a cursory glance. "Mother, she's here. Can we leave now?"

"I'm coming," called Lady Sheffield, stepping into the hall from the drawing room, where she had been inspecting her feathered headdress. "Really, it was too bad of Monsieur Fragonard to put such long feathers in this. I told him it was for a more casual occasion."

"You can let Rebecca fix it when we get there," said Claire. "You know how clever she is with such matters."

"Now, why didn't I think of that? Thank you, my dear. And may I say how wonderful you look tonight? Don't you think so, boys?"

The two gentlemen were accustomed to Lady Sheffield's propensity to regard them as boys despite their proximity to thirty years of age, so they didn't argue and only made suitable comments as they ushered the two ladies out the front door and down the steps to the waiting carriage.

Rebecca's town house in Mayfair was lit from top to bottom, and they had to wait in a line of carriages before descending at the front door. As usual, Rebecca's "little card party" would be the card party of the year.

The realization that this would be no small affair threw Claire back in time to that brief Season at the age of eighteen when she had grown accustomed to Society's palpable dismissal of her as someone of consequence. She had always known her sisters and brother were beautiful, but she had never realized how far short of the mark she fell until London's *ton* had shown her. Then grandmother's sudden death had forced them to leave London. Though she had been genuinely saddened by her grandmother's death, she had been inordinately relieved to end that dreadful Season.

Blindly, Claire took the arm offered her as they ascended the steps to the front door, steeling herself for the beginning of her worst nightmare, being brought forward to meet countless strangers and seeing the disappointment in their eyes when she was produced instead of another tall, dazzling Sheffield.

"Chin up, my dear. It's not as bad as that," whispered Kit, patting her hand as he leaned down, his tall, lean body sheltering her from the worst of the curious glances. "I'm here."

Claire smiled up at him, grateful for this kindness. With Kit by her side, perhaps things would be different this time. That was nonsense, of course. Kit would not always be by her side; it was not his place to perform such an office. Still, she would shine this night for his sake. She would show him his faith in her was not misplaced.

"Claire, you look wonderful!" exclaimed Lord Northam, her brother-in-law, holding out his hands and pulling her away from the safety of Kit's arm. "Come with me. I want to introduce you to some people."

"Northam, really, you needn't bother," she began.

"Oh, yes, needs must," he said, grinning down at her. "Else your sister will take me to task. Besides, it will be a pleasure to introduce my little sister-in-law to some of my friends. I daresay you will not have met them before. They are the sort who prefer political debates to social soirees."

As he spoke, he propelled her toward a knot of young people deep in conversation. Claire pasted her best social smile on her face and greeted each one in turn.

"And finally, this is Miss Hortense White and her brother, the Honorable Cyril White."

"How do you do, Lady Claire?" said the young woman, her eyes kind and warm, peering intently at the newcomer from behind a nose of rather astonishing proportions.

"Very well, Miss White. I am delighted to make your acquaintance, all of you," Claire added, including everyone in her smile.

"You must be the sister-in-law," said Mr. White. "Another of the Sheffield beauties, it is easy to see."

"Why, thank you, Mr. White," she responded, relaxing in the warmth of his lie. She had never seen any physical resemblance between her and the rest of her family—except old Aunt Gussie, whose moustache was the same shade as Claire's mousy hair.

"And Lady Claire is quite as clever as the rest of her clan," said Lord Northam.

"Then we shall have to be on our toes," commented a young man with coal black hair and a pale complexion. "Tell me, Lady Claire, are you a Tory or a Whig?"

"Must I be one or the other? I . . . I find much to admire in both parties." Claire was surprised at the ripple of shock manifested on their faces and decided immediately to continue this vein of conversation. Perhaps she would become the Sheffield who would shock everyone with her terribly wise and pithy comments.

"Amazing how you can insult both groups with one

simple statement, my lady," said the young man, a fanatical gleam in his eyes.

"Steady on, Dempster," said Mr. White.

"I don't mean to insult anyone, my lord. I simply mean that neither party holds all the answers."

"For instance?" demanded the passionate young man.

"Well, we all know the Tories are to be admired for making certain the war against the French ended well, but what has happened now that it is over? The soldiers who fought so gallantly, what has been done for them since Waterloo?"

"Hear, hear," said Mr. White, turning to the man with the glittery eyes. "What say you to that, Lord Dempster?"

"And what would you have Parliament do, my lady? Bankrupt the country by paying soldiers to rest on their, uh, laurels?"

"No, my lord, but a man must be able to provide for his family. Surely you must agree upon that point?" said Claire, her own tone turning passionate.

"Ah, I see we have a radical in our midst," said Miss White, her large nose wrinkling as she smiled.

"Not at all, but . . ."

"My lords, ladies, and gentlemen, Lord and Lady Northam are pleased to announce the opening of Northam Club. You may now adjourn to the card room, where play will begin," announced the butler, causing a general exodus among the group.

Though no one exactly escorted her, Claire was swept along with her new acquaintances toward the ballroom, which her sister had transformed into an elaborate gaming room. Above the double doorway, she had even had a gilded sign proclaiming the ballroom "Northam Club." Within, she had arranged a table for hazard, others for vingt-et-un, lansquent, commerce, and silver loo.

Smaller tables were scattered around the room for guests who preferred more intimate games of whist or piquet.

"You ought to feel right at home, Dempster," said Mr. White. "Looks rather like our club."

"Just you remember this is Lord Northam's home," cautioned Miss White.

Claire shook her head when she saw it. Rebecca never did anything by half measure. Dressed in white wigs and wearing lace at their collars and wrists, her footmen supervised the tables, making certain everyone was supplied with drinks.

"Quite a hostess, your sister," said Miss White. "What shall we play?"

"I don't do well at cards," admitted Claire.

"I would deem it an honor if you would allow me to show you how to play hazard, my lady," said Miss White's brother.

"Shall we?" Claire asked Miss White, who nodded.

They made their way to the hazard table, where her brother was throwing the dice. Kit was there, too, a fact that made the hazard table all the more attractive to Claire.

"Now, let me explain," began Mr. White. "Lord Sheffield will throw the dice. One adds the dice together; it will be a number between five and nine. Ah, the number is six this time. Everyone places his bet and the next throw is made."

"And what skills are involved?" asked Claire.

"Skill? Why, none, I suppose. It is entirely up to chance how the dice will fall."

Claire wrinkled her nose and said, "Perhaps we can play something else. I may not be very good at cards, but at least I know I am losing through my own ineptitude, not simply because of chance."

Mr. White chuckled and led her and his sister to the table where Speculation was being played, a game of little skill but one at which Claire felt comfortable losing. Sitting between the brother and sister, she was able to have a little conversation with them. By the end of the second round, she had lost ten shillings, while Mr. White had won almost as much.

"You know, Lady Claire, if you will just pay attention to the cards that have been played, you will know when to bid for the high card," he explained patiently.

"You are very kind to worry about me, Mr. White, and if I cared to win, I would pay closer attention. However, I prefer conversation with my friends to studying a deck of cards," she said, giving him a smile that made him blush. "I hope you will not be too disappointed in me."

"No, no, of course not, my lady. I did not mean to criticize you."

"I assure you I took no offense, Mr. White. Indeed, I am quite grateful to you, and to your sister, for making my evening so pleasant."

The young man stammered a reply and ducked his head, concentrating on his cards.

By the end of an hour, Claire was thoroughly bored with the entire evening—both cards and conversation. She should have spoken up when Rebecca mentioned cards. She had never enjoyed playing, and since she'd made Mr. White blush, his conversation had become forced and self-conscious. Miss White was affable, but she was too wrapped up in her brother's political career to be considered lively.

The first of many such glittering evenings, thought Claire, excusing herself from the company.

She wandered out of the ballroom in search of solitude and sanity. Her two nieces, Sophie and Pammy, would already be in bed, so she couldn't disturb them. Northam's library, which held countless fascinating volumes, was the obvious refuge—if no one else had discovered it.

Shuttling past the ballroom again, Claire hurried down the hall to the library, slipped inside, and shut the door.

"Did you get lost?" asked a familiar male voice.

"Kit! What are you doing in here?"

"I was just looking for something to read. More to the point, what are you doing in here? This evening was organized to give you a chance to meet new people."

"You mean gentlemen," she said, walking to his side and taking the book he held. "*Pride and Prejudice*? Oh, it's by Miss Austen."

"Yes. I have read it before, but I thought I might go back to some of the better passages. You had better return to Rebecca's little gambling hell before someone comes looking for you," he said.

"Hopefully, Rebecca will be too busy playing the hostess to notice, and you know Mother. Once she starts playing whist, the world does not exist."

"And Regina?"

"Oh, she wasn't feeling well, so she and Melton stayed home tonight."

"I see. Then there's nothing for it. You must stay in here and listen to Miss Austen's tale. Let's make ourselves comfortable."

They settled on the long, leather sofa, Kit at one end facing her, and Claire sitting at the other, her feet tucked under her stylish silk gown.

"It is a truth universally acknowledged that a single man in possession of a good fortune must be in want of a wife.

However little known the feelings or views of such a man may be on his first entering a neighborhood, this truth is so well fixed in the minds of the surrounding families that he is considered as the rightful property of some one or other of their daughters."

Claire chuckled. "I believe Miss Austen must have been watching Littlefield when Northam took up residence there."

"Shh, minx. Someone may hear you," said Kit, admonishing her with a wag of his finger.

Claire put her finger to her lips and said, "Continue."

Twenty pages and an hour later, Claire was quite caught up in the social tug of war between Miss Elizabeth Bennet and Mr. Darcy.

When Kit closed the book, she said, "Oh, please do not stop. I had no idea Miss Austen was such an excellent storyteller. It is something I wish I could do."

"You aspire to writing novels, Claire?"

"No, no. I tried when I was younger, but they were really quite horrid. But this is rather like listening to a friend tell a tale. I think it is wonderful how a story with such ordinary characters can be made so interesting— much more interesting than my life," Claire added with a sigh.

"Ah, yes. Speaking of your life, I have kept you to myself long enough. Like Miss Bennet, you have obligations to meet."

She rolled her eyes and pursed her lips. "I don't think there is a Mr. Darcy for me, Kit. I have met a Lord Dempster, Mr. White, and several other people whose names I have already forgotten."

"I am acquainted with Mr. White, an unexceptional fellow."

"And tongue-tied after I offered him the most bland compliment."

Kit's laughter rumbled forth. "But the gentlemen are supposed to offer you compliments, my dear girl, not the other way around."

"Then someone had better explain the rules to these gentlemen, because I do not think they were paying the least attention. Oh, Kit, this is so . . ."

"So early in the Season," he said, rising and pulling her to her feet. "You must give it time. I know your sister meant well, inviting all of Northam's political cronies, but I can see you want more frivolity in your evenings."

"Frivolity?" she said, giggling at his nonsense. "I assure you I do not want frivolity. I want someone who can talk about more than Parliament and gaming."

"Now, now, do not give up yet. Wait until you have met some of the other young men at Regina's dinner and theater party on Thursday. You do like the theater, don't you?"

"Of course I like the theater," she replied. "Don't you remember all those childish theatricals I would make you pay a shilling to watch?"

"Yes, and half the time you made me participate in them, too. Quite the bully, you were."

"As if a child of six could bully a boy of fourteen."

"But you did. You'd threaten tears, and there is absolutely nothing more terrifying to a member of my sex than to see a female, even a girl of six, cry." He gave a shudder, making Claire dissolve into giggles just as they reentered the ballroom.

Rebecca was watching, her brow raised in patent disapproval. She hurried to their side, taking Claire's hand and pulling her away from Kit.

"If this is how you intend to help find Claire a

husband, Lord Kittridge, it would be better that you do nothing at all."

"I beg your pardon, my lady. Lady Claire and I happened upon each other after seeking a moment of, uh, privacy. I had no idea you were looking for your sister."

"Very well. Claire, come with me. I want you to meet Lord Randall. I think you will be quite charmed by him. He's a particular protégé of Northam's."

Claire cast a long-suffering sigh, which led Kit to whisper, "Give the fellow a chance, CeeCee."

"Come and see what has arrived for you, my dear," exclaimed Lady Sheffield, waving a card at Claire on Tuesday morning. "A bouquet of flowers and this card, not to mention all the invitations we received in the morning post."

"Mother, the invitations would have arrived anyway. And the flowers? We do not even know they are for me. You probably have some secret admirer."

"Pish-tush, your name is the one on the envelope. Open it."

Claire opened the white envelope and pulled out a card decorated with watercolor pink flowers and scraps of lace. Her color heightened as she read the poem on the back.

"Who is it from?" demanded her mother.

Claire handed her the letter. "It says only *an admirer,* and the poem is nothing special."

"Nothing special? Why, it says right here he is counting the hours until he can be by your side again. Oh, I wonder which one of them sent it? And the rose, a perfect white rose. How romantic!"

"Good morning, Mother!" called her son, striding

into the breakfast room and helping himself to the array of dishes on the sideboard. "What's that? Something for the brat?"

"Robert, must you be so rag-mannered to your sister? If you must know, this card and rose arrived this morning. And the bouquet of flowers, too."

"From Mr. White," said Claire, making a moue.

"And who sent that, the card and white rose?" asked her brother casually, stuffing his mouth with pigeon pie.

"A secret admirer," said his mother. "The first of many, I'll be bound."

"I fail to see what use a secret admirer is to me. If he hasn't the . . . the good sense to identify himself, then how am I to thank him properly, or even to appreciate him for his thoughtfulness?"

"But it is for St. Valentine's Day, my dear. A time of romance," said her Mother. "Only tell her, Robert, how romantic it is."

"Pray do not ask me to explain romance," said the earl, diving into his food with relish.

"Oh, you are no help at all. And do not tell me you have not been eying that Miss Phipps." Her son ignored her comment and kept his head down. "Now, Claire, you must try not to be so very practical."

"I shall try, Mother, but right now, I must excuse myself if I am to make it to my fitting."

"Oh, your fitting! I cannot wait to see you in that gown. Shall I accompany you, dear?"

"No, you needn't bother. Nellie will do so."

"Very well, enjoy your morning. Oh, and if you go to Monsieur Fragonard's, do please mention that headdress to him."

"Yes, Mother."

When the footman had closed the door behind her daughter, Lady Sheffield turned to her son and demanded,

"Whatever were you thinking, cutting up one of my old cards from your father?"

Choking, it was a moment before Lord Sheffield could respond. "How the devil did you know?"

"When a particular young man paints a picture of pink roses because he is too poor to afford them, but he knows they are his intended's favorite, then a young lady remembers."

"I'm sorry, Mother. Kit and I . . ."

"Kit was in on this, too?"

"It was his idea."

"And what idea was that?"

"Kit thinks all Claire needs is a bit of confidence. He says she'll be every bit as successful as Reggie and Becca, but she doesn't see it. We thought we would invent a secret admirer to help coax her out of her shell."

"I see," said the matriarch, tapping the table with the card. "Not a bad idea, not bad at all, though I think we will have to do better than a single card."

"I am sorry about your card," said her son.

"Never mind the card, Robert. If it will help our sweet Claire shine, then it is well worth the cost."

"That's almost exactly what Kit said, but judging from the way Claire was acting, she was not terribly impressed."

"But it was only one card, Robert. What if she continues to receive cards, flowers, and little gifts? Something in her Valentine box every day. Even Claire will have to acknowledge she has at least one admirer. It must be the same handwriting, of course. Will you tell Kit?"

"Just leave everything to us, Mother."

"Thank you, Robert. Oh, and do tell Kit to purchase his own stationery."

"So I shall," replied Robert. "I'm very relieved you are not angry about it."

"Not at all, my dear boy. Now, I must run along," said Lady Sheffield, kissing the top of her son's head as she passed his chair. By the trestle table in the hall, she paused, looking thoughtfully at the row of heart-shaped boxes. Her lips curved slightly.

"What harm could it do?" she said.

"I beg your pardon, my lady," said Gravely, the butler.

"What? Oh, nothing. I . . . I will need the carriage brought around in a half an hour, Gravely. I will be calling on my other daughters this morning."

On Thursday evening, when they entered the private box at the theater, Claire felt a tremor of excitement run up and down her spine. Gazing across the wide theater, she wondered if her admirer were present, too. Was he looking at her while she studied the crowd? She clutched her reticule, which held the delicate lace handkerchief he had sent that morning. Perhaps during the interval she would stroll along the corridor with the handkerchief in her hand, touching her nose from time to time. If he saw her carrying his gift, surely he would come forward.

"Sit up front, Claire, so you can see," said her mother.

"And so I can be seen," she muttered, but she took the empty chair all the same.

Her sisters sat on either side of her, and Claire could not help but wish they had not done so. It was rather like placing a well-loved but battered book between two golden bookends. The thought made her sink lower in her seat. She certainly didn't want her secret admirer to make that particular comparison.

Then Claire forgot her worries when she heard the

voice that never failed to lift her spirits. She turned a
dazzling smile on Kit as he took the chair behind hers.

"Good evening, CeeCee," he whispered, his warm
breath teasing her neck.

"Good evening, Kit. I didn't know you were attending the play tonight."

"Oh, yes, never miss it," he said, resting his gloved
hand on the back of her chair. "And how are you ladies
this evening?"

"Very well," chimed her sisters, beaming at him as if
they shared some secret.

Claire frowned and made a mental note to ask Kit
about it later. Just then, the curtain rose, and she was
quickly lost in the make-believe world of Sheridan's *The
Rivals* and the hilarious misunderstandings of Mrs. Ma-
laprop.

When the curtain fell to signal the intermission,
Claire heaved a satisfied sigh and leaned back in her
chair, nearly jumping out of her skin when her back
touched Kit's hand.

"I beg your pardon," she said, blushing to the roots of
her mousy hair.

"No harm done," he replied softly, grinning down at
her in a brotherly fashion. He added, "Do you think we
might stroll . . ."

"Certainly not," hissed Rebecca, leaning between
them. "The young gentlemen will have spotted Claire in
Regina's box; she cannot disappear just as they begin to
seek her out."

"Thank you for asking, Kit," said Claire, looking
past his broad shoulders and seeing Mr. White's head
appear. The shy young man hurried forward, and Kit
rose, giving others the opportunity to claim her attention.

Kit wandered out to find some sort of refreshments,

accepting the lemonade and allowing Robert to add to its contents from his flask.

"To the ladies," said the earl, watching a particular bird of paradise over the rim of his glass.

"Humph," grumbled his friend.

"By the way, my mother recognized the pink rose on the card."

"Cut up stiff, did she?"

"No, she thinks your idea is quite clever. As a matter of fact, she wants you to continue."

"I have already done so," said Kit, wondering how Claire had liked the lace handkerchief he had sent.

"Good. I thought I might write a card or two myself."

"You don't want to go too far, Robert."

"No, but surely two admirers would be more convincing than one."

"It's not as if Claire won't have some real admirers, too," protested Kit. "She is quite a taking little thing, and we should not sell her short, you know."

"Nothing like that. Just a bit of help, a bit of a push. You'll see. She'll blossom like a . . . a . . . flower. I say, isn't that Belinda Duprey? I thought old Crutchaven had taken her to the Continent."

"Didn't you hear? The beautiful Belinda returned from Paris alone. Crutchaven keeled over dead in a deuced awkward position."

"That's what comes of old men and young women," said the earl, nodding at the lady in question. She gave him a smile. "So Belinda is in need of protection. I think I might have a word with her. Make my excuses to the family. You'll see them home, I trust."

"My pleasure."

Kit ambled back to the boxes. He had no trouble finding Lady Melton's box, but entering it was impossible. Not only had Mr. White and his sister joined them—

Miss White now occupied his chair—but three other young men hovered in the back of the box. In the back, Lord Randall also waited his turn with Claire.

"Evening, Randall," said Kit.

"Kittridge. Don't suppose you could get me closer to Lady Claire—being almost a member of the family, I mean."

Kit threw up his hands in mock defeat. "You see where I stand," he added. "I have even lost my seat."

"I suppose you know the Lady Claire rather well—as a brother."

"Yes, as a brother. And as such, I warn you, I do not bandy her name about." Black eyes met clear blue in perfect understanding.

"No need. I was only going to ask if she likes roses."

Kit ground his teeth before giving Randall a tight smile. "And what young lady does not?"

The next act was about to begin, and the box began to clear as everyone returned to his original seat. Kit slipped in behind Claire. He couldn't help but notice that her cheeks were quite pink, and her dark eyes sparkled like diamonds.

Kit frowned. He wasn't at all certain he agreed with his friend. Claire seemed to be coming out of her shell rather nicely without any further help from counterfeit admirers.

January came to a chilly end, and February blew through the streets of London, bringing cold and snow. Claire welcomed the snow, hoping it would slow the torrent of invitations, but nothing could stem the tide. Sitting in the drawing room, wrapped in a woolen throw to ward off the chill, she moaned as her sisters and mother combed through the growing pile, choosing those invitations that promised the greatest access to the largest number of eligible suitors.

Claire did her best to ignore them, replying to questions with noncommittal grunts while she devoured another of Miss Austen's novels. They were not quite as satisfying without Kit to read them out loud, but in her mind she could still hear his pleasing voice.

"Another card and flowers have arrived for Lady Claire."

"Thank you, Gravely," she replied, accepting the card from the butler. He placed the small bouquet of delicate lavender on the table beside her.

"Aren't you going to open the card?" asked Regina when Claire began reading her novel again.

"What? No, I know what it says."

"You know, Claire, there are those who might consider your disinterest a sign of snobbery," said her eldest sibling.

"If you want to read it, Rebecca, I give you permission to open it."

"No, no. I wouldn't dream of doing so."

"My dear, why don't you just see who sent them."

Claire tore into the envelope, quickly digested its contents and set it aside.

"It is from another *admirer*. After a while, you would think my admirers would want to take credit for all the flowers, poems, and gifts. Since they cannot be bothered to confess their affection, then I cannot be bothered to care."

"I beg your pardon, my lady, but another parcel has arrived."

Claire sat up straighter, taking the yellow envelope with trembling fingers. Her audience watched in interest as she read the card and then eagerly tore into the package. She pulled out a white wool scarf, holding it to her cheek and relishing its soft texture against her skin.

"You don't seem quite as indifferent to this secret admirer," said Rebecca.

"That's because . . . well, this one is different," said Claire.

"And why is this one different, my dear?" asked her kind mother.

"Because . . . because this was . . . well, there is something very sincere about this one's notes." Flushing uncomfortably, Claire picked up the scarf and card and left the room.

"Whatever is the matter, Mother?"

Lady Sheffield forced herself to return to the task at hand, saying, "Nothing, nothing at all. I only hope our little Claire finds someone soon. I will not feel comfortable until she has found someone like you two girls did."

"How could she not, here in London? By summer, we will all be planning Claire's wedding. You mark my words," said the sunny-natured Regina.

Card parties, musicales, literary readings, political evenings, dinners, and the theater. Life was already a whirl, and the Season hadn't even begun yet. Unfortunately, there had been no balls, no dancing yet. Lady Rigsby's ball was to be the first, and Claire felt a tremor of expectation every time she looked at the pale green gown. She hoped her admirers would take the opportunity of a waltz to make themselves known to her.

One thing was certain: all her admirers, both secret and open, were a generous lot. Mr. White, who always signed his cards, sent her flowers and bonbons regularly.

Lord Dempster, who always sought her out, called almost every day and sent flowers once. Lord Randall was also quite attentive, though he hadn't sent any flowers—a fact that made Claire wonder if the flowers from one of her secret admirers were not really from him.

It was one week until Lady Sheffield's St. Valentine's Day ball, and Claire was growing impatient to discover the identities of her secret admirers. Each morning when she checked her little heart-shaped box, there was always something new to make her smile.

Claire began to wonder why she had dreaded the Season so. There had been none of the awkwardness she remembered from her brief Season two years before. Her only trivial objection at the moment was that her curiosity was near to bursting. In her writing desk upstairs, she had stuffed cards from at least five different "secret admirers." She was growing impatient to discover their identities.

Claire was especially anxious to meet the first one, the one who had sent the card with painted roses. There was something different about him. His poetry was not flowery; his notes were not full of wild praise. Instead, his words were gentle and sincere, written in a bold hand that inspired confidence. The author of those notes was the sort of man she had always dreamed of. She was certain he was a man of integrity, she knew he possessed great wit, and his quotations from literature pronounced him a man of superior learning. This admirer was the sort of man with whom she could easily envision spending her life.

Claire knew it was stupid. The man might be anyone—someone totally unsuitable. But she couldn't convince herself of this. No, her true admirer was suitable for her in every way.

If only he would come forward and claim her.

*   *   *

"You look very beautiful tonight, Lady Claire," said Lord Dempster, after bowing to her at Lady Rigsby's ball.

Claire was suitably gratified to hear this compliment. Lord Dempster, with his brooding Byronic looks, was quite a conquest—if she had conquered him. She remained in doubt about that; all he ever wanted to do was talk about politics. She suspected he merely enjoyed using her as sounding board for his political rhetoric.

"Thank you, my lord," she responded after dipping a curtsy.

"Might I have the honor of this dance?" he asked, and again Claire smiled.

"Thank you. I would like that," she said, taking his arm and strolling onto the marble floor of the Rigsby ballroom.

She had feared—irrationally, perhaps—that she would sit idly by while all the other ladies danced every set. Instead, she had not had a moment alone.

"Have you seen Mr. White this evening?" asked Lord Dempster, his lips twitching.

"No, I'm afraid I haven't seen him."

The music began, a waltz, and he swept her into the steps of the dance. Claire reflected that she fit rather well with Lord Dempster, who was small in stature. Though his dress and manners were usually offhand and casual, his dancing was perfection itself, and Claire found herself relaxing in his arms.

"Just keep your eyes open. You cannot possibly miss Mr. White. I mean, you know I do not subscribe to any particular mode of dress, to the whims of fashion, and I thought my friend was like-minded in that."

"And now you think he is not, my lord?" said Claire.

"Well, I . . . only look. There he is."

"Oh, my," said Claire, turning away from the spectacle of the usually conservative Mr. White dressed in a black coat, spotted tie, and yellow pantaloons.

"Exactly!" said her partner, sniggering. "What a coxcomb he is. I should have known, though. I mean, he claims to be a Tory, but his sentiments are decidedly Whig—rather like yours, Lady Claire."

"I beg your pardon."

"No, no, I think none the less of you. You are, after all, only a lady, and your heart rules your mind. Mr. White, however, is another case entirely. I mean, the fellow spoke in favor of some wild plan to pay former soldiers to learn new trades."

"That does not sound so wild," said Claire, her eyes narrowing as her ire rose.

Lord Dempster had the audacity to chuckle and pat her back where his hand rested. Claire's heel came down squarely on the top of his foot, and he jumped back, causing her to miss her next step entirely. A few stumbles, and they were back on track, but Lord Dempster was frowning at her mightily and said not another word until the music had ended.

Taking her hand and placing it stiffly on his arm, he promenaded her around the room, stopping in front of Mr. White, who greeted them both warmly.

"Good evening, my lady, my lord," said the earnest young man, preening slightly.

"Good evening," replied Claire, not knowing where to look.

"What do you think?" he asked eagerly. "I know it is daring, but I went to a new tailor, and he assured me this was all the crack."

"It is . . . uh, quite colorful, Mr. White," said Claire.

Looking beyond him, she asked brightly, "Where is Miss White tonight?"

"Our younger brothers and sister have all contracted the chicken pox, and since Hortense has already had that ailment, she has gone home to help our mother. I stayed in town by myself," he added proudly.

"So she was not here to help you choose your new suit," said Claire.

"Obviously, *Miss* White is the one with taste," said Lord Dempster, not bothering to hide his amusement.

Mr. White frowned, cocking his head to one side, his nostrils flaring. "If you do not like my new coat, my lord, you have only to say so."

"I'm sure Lord Dempster is only wishing to know the name of your tailor," said Claire hastily.

She had no desire to see her two swains swapping challenges. Everyone would think she was the root of their quarrel. Nervous laughter bubbled up at the thought that two men might ever duel over her. Both young men faced her, their brows raised.

"I beg your pardon, gentlemen. I have the most shocking tendency to giggle when I am nervous. Please, for my sake, do not quarrel. The music is beginning again, and I don't even have a partner for this set," she said, gazing at Mr. White, forcing him to turn away from Lord Dempster and ask her to dance.

As they crossed the floor, what Claire really wanted to do was disappear. Every eye in the ballroom was staring at Mr. White's bright yellow pants. He was making a cake of himself, and of her, too, but he was completely oblivious to this fact. Recalling Rebecca's strictures, Claire managed a smile as they took their places for the quadrille.

To her dismay, Lord Dempster quickly secured his own partner and joined their square, directly opposite them. Claire heard Mr. White suck in a deep breath, and then the music began. There was no escaping now.

The figures of the dance required the two couples to meet in the middle. Lord Dempster looked pointedly at Mr. White's yellow pantaloons and whispered to his partner, who giggled. Claire glared at them both, but they ignored her completely. Mr. White's breathing grew more labored each time they met, until the final Demi Tour.

"I am not afraid to meet you, Lord Dempster," growled Mr. White in passing.

"Please," whispered Claire.

"Do you want to meet me?" said Lord Dempster.

"If that is what you want," said Mr. White.

"I want it if you do," replied Lord Dempster, stopping in the middle of the square.

The other two couples gaped while Mr. White and Lord Dempster butted chests.

"For heaven's sake, gentlemen! It is only a hideous pair of yellow pantaloons!" hissed Claire, tugging at Mr. White's arm ineffectively.

"Stand back!" demanded Mr. White, thrusting her aside and putting up his fists.

"You popinjay!" declared Lord Dempster, swinging wildly at his former friend, who was agile enough to duck.

Claire, however, was caught unawares. Lord Dempster's fist connected with her chin and spun her around. Furious, Claire attacked, balling up her fist the way Kit had taught her years before and striking Lord Dempster first, and then Mr. White for good measure. She would have continued her attack, but she was lifted bodily off the floor and carried away.

Scandalized, appalled, dismayed, angry—the emotions washed over her like a giant wave, sucking her deeper into despair.

Suddenly, she was upright again, looking into the faces of her savior—Kit—and her astonished mother and sister. She was vaguely aware of her brother-in-law's face, but she had too much information to digest already, and burst into tears.

They comforted her, cooing at her as if she were a child. Then the door opened—she wasn't quite sure where they had stashed her—and her brother's voice echoed in her ears.

"The carriages are outside. I have your cloaks, and I have made our apologies to Lady Rigsby."

Claire groaned, leaning against Kit's broad shoulder as they led her away.

"What the deuce is going on? It looks like a demmed hothouse!" declared the Earl of Sheffield, edging past a basket of flowers. "Did someone die?"

"Pray, do not be facetious, Robert," said Lady Sheffield. "Join us while we decide what is to be done."

"Wasn't our little Claire, was it? Dying of embarrassment?"

Claire lifted her face and glared at him.

"By Jove, that's quite a bruise you have there, little sister. Kit!" he called. "Come in here, if you can get past the forest."

Claire wanted to sink through the floor, but she refused to give her brother the satisfaction of cowering before his teasing. Besides, she wanted to see Kit and thank him for rescuing her.

Kit slipped into the room, taking a chair and pulling it close to Claire, studying her a moment, lifting her chin and nodding his head.

"Quite a prize, my dear. Quite a prize," he said, winking at her and taking her hand in his. He kept it there, much to Claire's delight.

"Will you two boys please quit teasing our Claire?"

"Yes, Mother," they said in unison.

"Really, this is a serious matter," said Rebecca, Lady Northam. "We have been discussing what measures to take to minimize the consequences of Claire's action. She has ruined her chances for a brilliant match, of course. No gentleman will want to ally his name with a hoyden."

Releasing Claire's hand, Kit turned slowly in his chair, staring down his aquiline nose at Rebecca until she squirmed in her seat.

"You know, Rebecca, I had never considered you an unfeeling person, but I take leave to tell you that was one of the most unkind things I have ever heard. You malign your sister who, as anyone of sense knows, did her best to defuse a volatile situation between two lob-cocks. It is hardly Claire's fault that things went awry.

"Thank you, Kit," said Claire.

"I'm sure I didn't mean to insult Claire. It was certainly not her fault that this debacle occurred, but I can tell you Society will have a heyday with this. Northam tells me the bets are already being taken as to when Dempster and Mr. White will meet, and everyone assumes Claire is the one they are fighting over—hardly a situation to add to her consequence."

"You and Northam don't give people much credit for good sense, do you, Rebecca?" commented her brother.

"I must say, Rebecca, I have to agree with Kit and Robert. Why, only look about you. Before Claire . . ." Lady Sheffield hesitated, searching for words to describe her daughter's actions.

"Screwed up their ogles," supplied Kit.

"Yes, well, before last night, Claire hadn't received half so many bouquets."

"Oh, she's received more than flowers," said Lord Sheffield, pausing for dramatic effect.

"What do you mean?" asked Lady Sheffield.

"I mean, Mother, that Lord Dempster called early this morning to offer his abject apologies and to offer for Claire's hand. How about that for planting him a facer?"

All eyes turned on Claire, whose eyes had turned to saucers, and whose mouth had dropped open.

"So, what do you say, little sister? He's quite a catch, I'm told. How should I answer him?"

"No," she breathed, glancing at Kit before giving a vehement shake of her head. "No, I . . . I can't. I . . . I won't!" Claire leaped to her feet and rushed from the room, startling everyone.

Then Kit grinned and said, "I always knew Claire had a great deal of sense! Now, if you'll excuse me, I have things to do." He kissed Lady Sheffield's cheek and nodded to Rebecca before strolling out of the room.

In the hall by the front door, standing before the trestle table lined with heart-shaped boxes, stood Claire. Kit placed a gentle hand on her shoulder, and she whirled to face him.

"It's just me, CeeCee. What's wrong?" He took out his handkerchief and wiped the tears from her cheeks. "Here, now blow," he instructed, holding the cloth to her nose.

Claire chuckled and shook her head. "I am not that much of a watering pot," she said.

"I am sorry Rebecca said what she did. Then there was Robert's little revelation. I am very glad you had the good sense to turn down Lord Dempster's offer."

"It's not that," she said, handing him a card written on yellow stationery. "Read this."

Kit didn't have to read it to know what it said. After all, he had written it. But he took it and skimmed it before handing it back to her.

"Another of your secret admirers," he quipped.

"No, not another one, the only one. I do not count the others. But this one . . . Kit, how can I possibly consider someone's else's offer of marriage when my heart is already taken?"

"But, Claire, this is just a letter, like all the other letters you've been receiving," said Kit.

Claire shook her head. "No, Kit. I know nobody else will understand, but I think I am falling in love with whoever has been writing these cards. I didn't realize it myself until Robert told me Lord Dempster had offered for me. I was attracted to him, I must admit. And he has been quite attentive, saying all the right things and giving me confidence . . ."

Kit winced at this. Hadn't that been his plan when he began writing her love letters?

"But, Kit, Lord Dempster is not the author of the yellow letters, as I call them, and I cannot possibly consider his suit, not when my heart may already be engaged for my secret admirer."

"I wish there were something I could say to help you, CeeCee," said Kit.

"There is. You can help me discover who is sending these cards. I had hoped he would come forward at the ball last night, but . . . Please, Kit, will you help me?"

"I don't see what I can do to help. I don't even live here. Maybe Gravely or one of the footmen . . ."

"Gravely insists he does not know how the letters arrive, who brings them, or anything."

"I see. Well, I still don't know what I can do."

Her shoulders sagged. "You're right. I am just grasping at straws. You have always helped me out of my scrapes. I guess I forgot you do have your limitations. Thank you anyway, Kit." She stood on tiptoe and kissed his cheek, giving his hand a squeeze before taking the yellow card and walking away.

Kit watched her until she was out of sight. His jaw muscles twitching furiously, he picked up his beaver hat and slammed out of the front door.

Mr. White retired to the country. Lord Dempster, who did not hold his liquor well, visited his club and informed everyone about his rejected suit. This, of course, Lord Northam related to his good wife, and Rebecca rushed to the Sheffield town home to air her dire predictions. Her counsel fell on deaf ears: Lady Sheffield's, because the volume of posies and gifts arriving for her youngest daughter continued to swell; and Claire's, because she simply did not care what society thought.

Frustrated, Rebecca sought solace from her other sister, but Lady Melton also failed to realize how dangerous was the road their little sister was on.

Spying Viscount Kittridge near Hatchard's lending library, Lady Northam decided to try for an ally one final time. Signaling her coachman to pull over, she opened the door to her carriage and summoned the handsome viscount.

"Good morning, Lady Northam," said Kit, standing beside the open door.

"Won't you ride a short way with me, Kit? I have something very particular to say to you."

"Very well," he replied, climbing inside and taking the rear-facing seat. He took in her worried frown and said "Nothing has happened to Claire, has it?"

"No, no, not like that. It is just this scandal. I cannot make Claire or Mother see the danger she is in."

"Hardly danger, Rebecca," said Kit, sitting back and smiling.

"Perhaps it is not physical danger, but it is danger, nonetheless. Everyone seems oblivious to the real peril—losing her reputation. Why, Lord Dempster is making a laughingstock of Claire. Northam says Claire's name is bandied about in the most shocking manner."

"Rebecca, that is nonsense. I have heard the talk, but none of it is ruinous. Indeed, people are realizing Dempster's obsession with our Claire has led him to behave in a bizarre manner. The man is ruining himself, both socially and politically."

"I don't give a fig about Dempster. He may go to perdition if he likes, and the sooner the better. It is Claire who concerns me."

Kit straightened on the velvet seat, watching as Rebecca mutilated the scrap of a handkerchief in her hands. Rebecca tended to be puffed-up in her own consequence, but she wanted only the best for her sister.

"Rebecca, what do you want me to do?"

"Have a talk with Claire. She has always listened to you, Kit. You can make her realize all these flowers she has been receiving, all the visitors, they are just curious, just interested in expanding the tale of her exploits."

Kit stiffened at her choice of words. Exploits? Claire didn't have exploits, and heaven knew she had done nothing to earn such an allegation. All Claire had ever wanted was to remain in the country. The entire Season was no more than an annoying, perhaps even frightening, obligation, a requirement for a young lady of her social status.

"Will you speak to her? At least warn her to be careful?"

"Very well, I'll have a word with her, but, Rebecca,

you must credit her with more common sense than to have her head turned by these people who are trying to turn this situation into something more than it is."

"Thank you, Kit."

When she had dropped him in front of his tailor's shop again, Kit entered with more in mind than his new coat.

"Good morning, my lord," said the clerk behind the counter. "Have you come for your fitting?"

"Good morning, Parker. No, I don't have time for that this morning. I need a little information. Lord Dempster is one of your customers, is he not?" The clerk nodded. "Do you happen to have his direction?"

"Why, yes, my lord. Just a moment."

Minutes later, Kit left the tailor's shop and headed toward St. James Street, where Lord Dempster kept a suite of rooms.

His knock was answered by a gray-haired major-domo, who took his card and disappeared. He returned and led Kit down a short, narrow hall to a large room with rich, plush furniture and a thick carpet underfoot.

"His lordship will be with you in a moment, my lord."

"Thank you." As Kit prowled the room, he was busy rehearsing the meeting to follow. He would give Dempster two seconds to agree to an abject, public apology to Claire, or he would flatten him like the little worm he was. With each turn of the room, his fury grew.

A door opened, and Kit whirled around, ready to pounce. He was taken aback by the pitiful figure that shuffled in. Dempster wore a silk banyan, its tie hanging loose and trailing on the floor. Beneath it, he sported knit breeches and a soiled shirt. One look at those dark eyes, and Kit guessed the cause for the young man's disarray.

"Kittridge, must apologize for my appearance. Appalling headache this morning. Be seated, won't you?"

Dempster fell into the nearest chair with a groan. Kit grabbed a nearby chair and picked it up, putting it down forcefully next to his host, who again groaned.

"What the devil do you mean, bandying about Lady Claire's name as if she were some sort of lightskirt?"

"I . . . I never," said the young man, his voice cracking and lacking conviction.

Dempster belched and sputtered, giving off the stench of stale gin. Kit sat back and shook his head.

"You are a mutton-headed toss-pot. You know that, don't you?"

"How dare . . . Oh, what do I care? Are you going to call me out? Go ahead. Much good it will do you. I can't even hold a pistol, much less fire one." He held up his right hand, which was heavily bandaged.

"What the devil is the matter with your hand?" demanded Kit, hoping it was something very painful.

"Mr. White and I finally went a round or two. He's not so awkward with his fives as he is in society."

"I could have told you that. Haven't you ever seen him at Jackson's Club?"

"Never go there m'self. Can't stand the thought of fighting—fists, pistols, swords, it's all the same to me. I hate them all equally and so am equally bad at them all."

"Then why the devil are you going around badmouthing Sheffield's sister? Don't you know his aim is perfect?"

"No, I didn't. Don't go to Manton's Shooting Gallery, either."

"Look, I'm telling you. Leave town for a while."

"Can't. I've got to speak in Parliament in two days. I can't go home until after the vote."

"Very well, but do not leave your lodgings unless attending a session at the House. And, Dempster, if I receive any reports that you have gone to the clubs or had so much as a thimble of gin at some other gathering, I will call you out, with Sheffield as my second. And when I'm done, he will call you out. Do you understand?"

"I understand."

"Good." Kit rose and strode to the door.

"Kittridge, please tell Lady Claire I did not mean to hold her up to public ridicule, that I still hold her in the . . . greatest . . ." His speech died beneath Kit's ferocious glare.

Without another word, Kit hurried out of the house, marching down the street, not looking to the left or right. Acquaintances hailed him, but he ignored them. His thoughts were absorbed with the problem that had presented itself the day after Lady Rigsby's ball.

Why the deuce should Claire's problems cause him such gnashing of teeth? She was like a sister to him, had been for as long as he could remember, anyway. He tried to picture himself getting so disturbed if Rebecca or Regina were suffering from some scandal. It was impossible to imagine. He felt certain they would garner nothing more from him than passing sympathy and some judicious words of wisdom.

Perhaps, he decided, his own role in this little theatrical was causing him such distress. When he had stepped into the hall and found her in tears, all because she wanted to learn the identity of her secret admirer, he had wanted to call himself out! What a cad he had felt!

Kit stopped in his tracks, gazing up at the façade of the Sheffield town home. In his reverie, he hadn't noticed his direction—had only been placing one foot in front of the other. Somehow, his steps had led him here.

How often he had come here in the past, his heart filled with gladness at the prospect of the welcome he would receive—the welcome of a cherished family member? He had sometimes taken it for granted, but now the enormity of this gift overwhelmed him.

Kit shook his head. Perhaps what astounded him the most, however, was that it simply wasn't enough—not anymore. Lady Sheffield might treat him like a second son. Robert certainly considered him a brother, as did Regina and even Rebecca. Hadn't Rebecca chosen him to come to Claire's rescue?

Claire.

He had betrayed the one member of the family whose loyalty and devotion had been unwavering. His heart constricted, the pain almost physical.

"Kit? What are you doing standing on the pavement like that? Are you coming in or are you not?" demanded Claire, her brown eyes dancing with amusement as she gazed down at him from the open door.

Kit smiled, hesitating only a moment while she stretched out her hand to him. Two at a time, he took the stairs, grasping her hand and following her inside.

His heart felt ready to burst.

Claire. Why hadn't he realized before? Claire was the one, the only one for him. She was smart and witty, strong and beautiful—more than he had ever hoped for, certainly more than he deserved.

"Look what someone has sent me," said Claire, releasing his hand and reaching down to pick up a trembling puppy. "Isn't he adorable? I am calling him Regent because he has such a regal face. Don't you agree?" she asked, holding the puppy's face with one hand while struggling to keep him in her arms.

Kit took the dog from her, holding him at arm's length and shaking his head. "Look at the size of those paws. By the time the Season is over, he will be bigger than this house."

"And so I told her," said Lady Sheffield, smiling upon them both from her chair in the drawing room. "But Claire will not listen to me. Perhaps you can talk some sense into her, Kit."

Tucking the puppy under his arm, Kit followed Claire to the sofa and sat down by her side. The puppy squirmed and wriggled until a quiet word from Claire made him still. Turning his head, the puppy licked Kit's face from chin to forehead.

"Oh, dear!" cried Lady Sheffield. "Do take that beast outside, Claire."

"Yes, Mama," she said, rising and leading Kit, his arms full of puppy, out of the room. Pausing by the back door to throw on a shawl, Claire smiled up at Kit and opened the door.

"I can take him from here," she said.

"No, I'll put him down outside. He's bigger than you are."

In the garden, Kit set him down, and the puppy stood between Kit's legs for a moment, assessing the situation.

"Let's go, Regent," said Claire, her voice setting him in motion. Laughing, she followed after the long-legged puppy as he gamboled along.

"He runs like a newborn colt," she called, chasing the dog through the garden paths, which were lined with small evergreen shrubs.

Kit watched them go, thinking that Claire and the puppy were very much alike. Claire was more graceful, to be sure, but she was every bit as uncomplicated and honest. And in a way, she was just finding her legs, too—her social legs.

There was that swelling again, his heart feeling ready to burst as he watched her pick up a stick and throw it in the air. It landed close to Regent, who yelped and galloped headlong to the safety of Kit's legs.

"Coward!"

"He just knows a safe haven when he sees one," said Kit, his black eyes shining as Claire returned to his side. He pulled a twig from her hair, his gaze resting on her lips for a moment. Her lips parted as time stood still.

Now was not the time. Swallowing hard, Kit said, "So you intend to keep this bruiser?"

"Certainly. I'm sure he will be much happier when the Season is over, and we can return to the country . . ."

"Just like you?" observed Kit.

"Yes, just like me. But you know, Kit, if I sent him home now, he would never truly be my dog. You must have them as puppies to make them your dog, do you not agree?"

"Certainly. Once you have earned the love and trust of any youngster, they will remain loyal forever."

"Exactly. So Mother will just have to put up with him."

"Which admirer sent him?"

"I'm not sure. I believe it was Blue Admirer."

"The blue admirer?" he asked, reaching down and scratching Regent's belly.

"Yes, there is the one who always writes on yellow stationery, the one who writes on white, and the one who writes on blue. I suppose they each bought only one box of stationery."

"And what will you do if they run out and begin using a different color?" he asked, straightening until he was looking down at her again.

"Silly, it is not only the stationery. It is the handwriting and the tone of the letters. Blue admirer always writes in very bad verse, but I think he is more sincere than White Admirer. White Admirer writes very good verse, but I suspect he copies them from some volume of poetry."

"And Yellow Admirer?" asked Kit, watching her color rise, until her cheeks were quite as pink as her gown.

"He is different. Sincere, I think, but perhaps he is only more practiced in the art of flirtation. I begin to wonder about all of them."

"And what do you wonder, CeeCee?"

She glanced away, and he thought she meant to put him off. Then she said softly, "I have come to believe that a true admirer would not take so long to make himself known to me. I fear they are all fickle."

"Perhaps not all of them," said Kit. "I thought you were falling in love with Yellow Admirer."

She shook her head, lifting her chin with an air of determination. "That was just foolishness. A girl cannot possibly fall in love with a phantom."

She shivered, and Kit took the opportunity to put his arm around her shoulder and guide her back to the house. Regent, ready for a nap by the warm fire, followed them inside.

"You are planning to come for dinner on Thursday, before the ball, are you not, Kit?" asked Lady Sheffield, who had moved to the escritoire and was writing something down.

"Certainly, my lady."

"Good. That will keep my numbers even. I am expecting forty people for dinner. At the ball, of course, there will be perhaps one hundred and fifty. Not a paltry number considering it is not yet March."

"Very impressive, Mama."

"I have included that very nice young lady, Miss Fetherston—the one with the blond hair. You are acquainted with her, are you not, Kit?"

"I have been introduced to her," he said cautiously.

"Good. I am trying to arrange the table, and I may have you lead her into dinner, since you have already been introduced."

"If that is what you need, my lady, I am at your service," said Kit, watching Claire to discover the slightest sign of jealousy.

She grinned at him and rolled her eyes, but all she said was, "Would you like some tea, Kit?"

"No, I really should be going," he replied, rising and strolling over to the escritoire to give Lady Sheffield a kiss on the cheek. Regent followed him to the door.

"Are you trying to steal my dog?"

"Please do," said her ladyship.

"No, Regent. You stay here. That's a good boy," he added when the puppy sprawled on the floor, gazing up at him with soulful eyes. "I'll come see you tomorrow."

"Good-bye, Kit," said Claire, who had knelt down beside Regent and was rewarded by a sloppy kiss.

The evening passed quietly for Claire—except for Regent's howling in the garden when he heard other dogs begin barking at the moon. Startled out of a deep sleep, she lay with pounding heart for a moment before recognizing the eerie sound. She waited a few minutes for the noise to subside, but when it didn't, she padded silently down the stairs and took the puppy back to her room, where he claimed the middle of the bed as his own. Claire hung onto the edge, wresting a small portion of the cover away from the greedy pup.

Wednesday dawned, and Claire awoke with a feeling of anticipation. Madame Celeste was to deliver her ball gown at eleven. In the afternoon, she had promised to help Cook make her sweets for the supper buffet for the ball the next night. Cook always asked for Claire's help, knowing full well her young mistress would eat as many as she could while working on them. The evening was a musicale at Lady Fetherston's, the mother of one of her school friends.

The morning unfolded precisely as Claire had anticipated. Her ball gown, a deep rose silk with simple lines and uncomplicated embellishments, was perfect. The dressmaker had fashioned tiny white silk roses to trim the sleeves and high waist. The kid gloves and slippers Claire had ordered matched the gown perfectly. All in all, Claire could feel her anticipation growing. She felt certain something of great import was going to happen at her mother's St. Valentine's Day Ball.

"I'm going to slaughter that dog!" shouted Cook, brandishing a large kitchen knife as she rushed into the garden.

Claire, who had taken Regent outside for some air, turned in horror as the large woman chased the puppy, who thought it was a wonderful game, down one cobbled aisle and up the next.

Catching the cook's arm, Claire whirled her around, demanding, "What has he done?"

"Eaten them, eaten every last one of them!"

"The sweets we spent all afternoon making?" gasped Claire. "I'll help you!" she shrieked, picking up her skirts and setting off in hot pursuit.

Panting and grumbling, Claire skidded to a halt when she encountered a broad chest in her pathway on the second trip around the walled garden.

"I understand Regent has been a naughty puppy," said Kit, chuckling at Claire, who glared up at him. Behind him, Regent bounced up and down like a ball, wagging his tail and barking. "You don't appear to be winning this one."

"I . . . I wanted to . . . kill him. Do you know what he did?"

"Yes, Cook told me. She is back in the kitchen, starting over."

"Oh, I feel so bad," said Claire, pushing her hair out of her face.

"I'll tell you what. I will stay here and help Cook while the rest of you go to the Fetherstons'. While I'm sure Madame Cataloni's performance will be inspiring, I always dread the other performers who are coaxed to have a go at singing."

"But I can't let you do that," said Claire.

"Yes, you can. You have to go, Claire."

"No, I don't. I should stay and help, too."

"Yes, I remember how much help you are. Cook has to fix twice as many just to have enough left for the ball after you have had your fill," said Kit, chuckling down at her as he led her back to the house.

"How very droll. But this time, I shan't want any of them. I had my fill this afternoon. Oh, I cannot believe he managed to ruin all of them. I must stay and help."

"But, Claire, you know how I hate to side with Rebecca, but you really should put in an appearance. You did not go anywhere last evening, and tonight if you do not show yourself, rumors will surface that you are in hiding."

"Oh, really, Kit, it cannot be as bad as all that. I mean, we will have over a hundred people in the house tomorrow night. That is hardly hiding."

"No, of course not, but if there is any . . . discomfiture, would it not be better to deal with it tonight, before your mother's ball?"

"Oh, very well, but I want you to come, too. We will

go inside and help Cook as much as possible, and then we will go to Lady Fetherston's together."

"Only if there is time," he replied.

They linked arms and entered the kitchens, where Cook put them to work peeling apples for her tiny bite-size tarts.

"Do be careful, my lord. You don't want to muss your coat," said Cook, tying a clean white cloth around his neck like a bib. Claire giggled and bowed her head, concentrating on the apple in her hands.

"I hope everyone sings off-key tonight," whispered Kit.

"Then I shall stuff cotton in my ears," she replied. "I must confess, I am looking forward to seeing Laura again. We were at school together, you know."

"No, I did not know. So you told your mother to pair me up with Miss Fetherston for supper tomorrow night?"

"Certainly not. If I had thought of it, I would have told Mother to pair you with me. It would make for a much more digestible meal than having, say, Lord Randall for a dinner companion."

"So Lord Randall will be here?"

"Of course. You know he is Northam's protégé; I met him at Rebecca's card party and have spoken to him several times since then."

"So you like Lord Randall?"

"He is tolerably good company," she said, "but I shan't be as comfortable with him as I could be with you. Besides, I think he just might be one of my secret admirers."

"Which one?" he asked, not daring to lift his gaze to meet hers.

"Oh, not Yellow Admirer. No, I think he might be Blue Admirer. I am not certain by any means, you know.

It is just a feeling I have. I was driving in the park with Rebecca on Saturday, and he suddenly appeared."

"Perhaps he was just out exercising his horse. We do not have many fine days for that at this time of the year."

She rolled her eyes and pointed to his apple, which lay on the table, forgotten. "Get busy, my lord, or Cook will never finish."

"Yes, my lady. At once, my lady."

Their teasing and laughter filled the quiet of the kitchens. Cook watched over them, an indulgent smile on her face. When Regent had the temerity to follow the pot boy inside, she even gave the puppy a soup bone and allowed him to lie beneath the big round table where Kit and Claire worked and chatted.

An hour passed in this companionable fashion, but then Claire's maid came to claim her.

"I will remain behind, slaving over a hot stove, so you may enjoy your musical evening, my lady. But in payment, I expect the first dance tomorrow night," said Kit.

"It will be an honor, good knight."

Rising, he made a production of bowing over her hand, kissing the back of it and getting flour all over his lips and the tip of his nose.

"How elegant you look, my lord," said Claire, reaching up and smearing the flour on his nose with her fingertip.

"No sacrifice is too great, my lady," he replied, reaching down and dusting his hands across the floury table. "I bid you good evening," he said, taking her face in his hands and patting it gently.

With a gurgle of laughter, Claire pushed him away and scampered out of the room. Under the table, Regent rose to follow, but Kit ordered him to stay, and he obeyed.

Petting the silky head that rested on his lap, Kit

muttered, "No reason you should be allowed in her room when I am not."

The day of the St. Valentine's Day ball dawned cold and drizzly. Claire woke with the headache and had to force herself to climb out of bed. The euphoric anticipation about the ball from the day before was replaced with uneasiness, though she knew of no reason her outlook should have taken such a drastic turn.

Sitting in the velvet-covered chair beside the fire, Claire clasped her cup of chocolate and reviewed the musicale evening at Lady Fetherston's house. She had received a great deal of attention, but no one had said a word about Lord Dempster. They had all been quite pleasant. Lord Randall had asked permission to take her for a drive in the park on the first fine day, and Claire felt a surge of relief that it would not be this day.

She did not believe in second sight. Certainly she did not possess it, being of too practical a nature, but she could not shake her uneasiness.

"I'm afraid that dog of yours has been at it again, my lady," said Nellie as she laid out a morning gown.

"Oh no, not the tarts again."

"No, it was your brother's kidney pie. He slipped into the breakfast room and stole it off the sideboard. Cook has banished him to the mews."

"I suppose that is for the best. We do not want him to upset Cook again—not today, of all days. I daresay no one could save him if he did it again."

"Will you be going out this morning, my lady?"

"No, I have the headache. I think I will stay in my room and read. I won't bother to dress until later. If my mother needs me, please send for me."

"Very good, my lady."

Claire settled deeper into the chair, her headache easing as she left the world around her for the countryside in Miss Austen's novel. By noon, she had finished the novel. Rising and stretching like a cat, she rang for her maid and ordered her bath.

Their guests would begin arriving at six for dinner. Regina and Rebecca would come even earlier to pass judgment on her appearance—not that she was concerned about that. The rose-colored gown was the prettiest thing she had ever owned. It was both elegant and simple. Wearing it, she knew she would have all the self-assurance she would need to survive the ball. And since her wooden heart on the trestle table in the hall was fairly overflowing with cards and little gifts, she had nothing to be ashamed of when the guests asked her to relate the story behind this unusual family tradition.

Her hair freshly washed and her bath complete, Claire began to get restless. She wished she had thought to select another book from the lending library. Then she remembered the slim volume Kit had brought her was in the library downstairs.

Shoving her feet into slippers, Claire tied her woolen dressing gown more tightly around her slender waist. No one would be downstairs except the servants. She had nothing to fear.

She paused at the landing, listening for any sounds that might indicate her brother was at home or that anyone had called. The tall case clock in the hall chimed two o'clock. Her mother, she knew, would be napping. Everything appeared quiet, and she tripped lightly down the stairs and down the short corridor to the library.

Picking up the book, *Shamela,* Claire started back to the door. Then, with an unladylike snap of her fingers, she remembered she needed to replenish the writing paper in her desk upstairs. Going behind her father's old desk, she sat down and opened the top drawer. Nothing but the household books in there. Then she opened the bottom drawer, and there was the extra stationery.

As she pulled it out, something under it fluttered to the floor. Claire reached for it, her hand slowing as she glanced at the writing on the card. The lines fairly leaped off the page: *I count the days until we can again be together, my love.*

With trembling hands, she studied the paper, the irregular tear on one edge. Turning it over, she could see wisps of pink watercolor. Clutching the card in her hand, she rose and made her way out of the library and down the hall, to the stairs.

"Lady Claire, another card has arrived for you. A yellow card," said the old butler, smiling kindly at his mistress.

Claire shook her head and pushed it away.

"My lady, are you all right? You look as if you have seen a ghost. Shall I help you?"

His questions were ignored as she dragged herself up the stairs and to her room.

Claire forced herself to go to the delicate writing desk and take out that first card, the one with the pink roses painted on one side. She shut her eyes, biting at her lower lip. Then she forced herself to open them and study the torn side of the card, comparing it to the paper that had fluttered to the floor.

The two ragged halves fit together perfectly.

Someone, someone in her own family, had written the card she had cherished so. Frowning, she pulled out all the cards written on the yellow stationery. The handwriting matched perfectly.

A sob caught in her throat. What had she said to Kit? Something about the admirer who wrote on the yellow stationary being more sincere. Why, she had practically declared her love for the person.

Pieces of the puzzle began to fall into place. Kit's expression of sympathy—pity was perhaps the better word. And then there had been her brother's shared smile with her sisters. Had Robert been in on the charade as well? And what of her sisters?

The past few weeks had been a lie, a farce. Not only did she not have a secret admirer, she didn't even have a family she could trust!

Anger replaced self-pity, and Claire set out to plot her revenge. It could not be physical, of course, but she would make them suffer in some manner. First, she would have to discover how many of them were involved. Had they all known?

"It is time to dress for dinner, my lady," said Nellie, entering the room, carrying Claire's ball gown.

Claire kept her own counsel while allowing her maid to arrange her hair and dress her. When she was pinned and taped, she gave a grunt of satisfaction.

"Thank you, Nellie."

"You're very welcome, child. How beautiful you look. Not like your sisters, of course, but every bit as beautiful."

Claire looked at the maid and smiled.

She then walked to the escritoire and took out all the notes—yellow, white, and blue.

Downstairs, she arrived in the salon before anyone else. She settled herself by the fire, the notes hidden in the folds of her skirt.

"Good evening, Claire. You look wonderful," said Northam, strolling into the room. "Rebecca told me you had ordered the perfect gown, and I can see she was right."

"Where is Rebecca?" asked Claire sweetly.

"Upstairs with your mother. Regina, too. Melton is seeing to the team."

The twins entered the room, chattering happily about the treat of watching the ball from the gallery and staying up until eleven o'clock. They tried to pull Claire to her feet to see her gown, but she refused to budge. Then Lady Sheffield entered the drawing room, and the twins clustered around their grandmother.

"Good evening, Claire, darling. What a delicious shade of rose," said Regina.

Claire thanked her sister, feeling a flicker of regret that Regina would be subject to the coming unpleasantness. If there was one person she didn't suspect, it was Regina. Rebecca, on the other hand, might very well be a part of the conspiracy—if there was a conspiracy.

"Hello, everyone," said the earl, entering the room and kissing his mother and then each of his sisters in turn. Then he pretended he was going to kiss his nieces, but tickled them instead. They were not amused.

"Uncle Robert, we are much too old for such nonsense."

"That's a fine way to greet your uncle. What is an uncle for, if not to tickle you and make you laugh?"

"But not tonight, Uncle. We are all dressed up and everything."

"So you are. I tell you, Northam, in four years, I do not envy you. You'll have more silly young men swarming around your house than bees to the honey pot."

"I know. The older they are, the more seriously I consider building a castle with a high tower and locking them in it."

"Papa!" the twins protested.

Rising from her chair, Claire cleared her throat.

"If I may have your attention," she said, clutching the notes in one hand. Everyone turned politely, and she added, "I want to know which one of you has been writing these notes."

"Claire, whatever are you talking about?" asked Regina.

She waved the papers and cards in the air, some of the slips floating to the floor. "These are supposed to be from secret admirers, but then, at least one of you knows better. Who is it?" She glanced from one face to the next, but was none the wiser. Every one of them looked to be racked with guilt.

"You may as well tell me."

"I'm afraid I asked Northam to write them," said Rebecca. "Mother thought it would help you gain a little confidence."

"Mother! You knew about this?" demanded Claire, reeling from this blow. "How could you?"

"It was just to give you confidence. And it worked like a dream! You have begun to shine like the diamond you are. Besides, I didn't know everyone was going to begin writing you notes," said Lady Sheffield.

"Well, I hate to contradict my wife, but I did not write all those notes," said Lord Northam. "Mine were white."

"And mine were blue," said Lord Melton, who had slipped into the room and stood behind his wife's chair. "Your mother asked me if I would send you a note or two, just to make you look forward to the coming Season. You seemed so glum about being here in London. I'm sorry, Claire. I didn't mean any harm."

"That leaves only the yellow ones, and you, Robert."

"I did not write those notes, Claire," replied her brother.

She glared at him, but he didn't even flinch. Her mother, however, looked away, and Claire groaned.

"Come and get them. Every one of them," she snapped, holding them out while her family came closer, sheepishly claiming their handiwork. She was left holding only yellow cards.

"Robert, do you swear these are not from you?" Claire demanded.

"On my word of honor, little sister," he said, grinning disarmingly. "It seems you have at least one true admirer."

"I find it hard to credit," said Claire, letting the papers fall to the floor. She marched to the doorway just as Gravely arrived to announce their first guests.

"You will make my excuses," she said.

"But Claire, you cannot mean . . ."

Her mother fell silent. Claire slipped out of the room and along the wall until she reached the obscurity of the back hall. Taking the servants' stairs, she gained the sanctuary of her room.

Her maid, who was tidying up, froze in surprise. "Are you ill, my child?"

"No. I am fine. Just leave me, please, Nellie."

"Very well, but if you want anything, anything at all . . ."

Claire shook her head, and the maid left her alone. She sat down on the bed, waiting for the tears to come.

What a fool she had been! And how foolish they had been! They thought so little of her chances for success that they had done their best to deceive her—her own family! And Robert, he had simply lied to her. He had to be the one who sent the first card with the roses. Someone had taken it out of the desk in the library. And that person had continued to write to her, switching to the yellow stationery. Robert was the only one who could have . . .

Claire gasped as another possibility revealed itself. What if Kit . . . No, she could not believe it. Not Kit, not her Kit. Did he, too, think so little of her chances?

Claire had never before wanted to run away from

home. Now, at the mature age of almost one and twenty, she found herself plotting to do just that!

Instead, she lay back on the bed, curling into a ball—unable to cry, unable to feel anything except the black well of despair.

"Good evening, Sheffields," said Viscount Kittridge, entering the drawing room on the heels of several other dinner guests. The replies were stiff, and he was about to question this unusual reception when Gravely walked past, carrying a small mound of yellow stationery. Kit followed the butler into the hall where he placed them on the table next to Claire's heart-shaped box. Frowning, Kit picked up the unopened note he had sent only that afternoon and slipped it into his pocket.

"What is all this, Gravely?" he asked, a worried frown creasing his brow.

"I couldn't say, my lord," came the stiff reply.

"Of course you can, Gravely. You and I both know where all these notes came from originally. What the devil are they doing in your hands now?"

"Lady Claire dropped them, my lord."

Kit turned back to the drawing room, but the butler stopped him, saying sadly, "Lady Claire has discovered that there were never any secret admirers. She is most distressed."

"Then I'll talk to her," he said, turning away again.

"Lady Claire has gone to her room, my lord. I do not think she wants to be disturbed. Her maid Nellie is in the kitchen crying."

"Blast! I . . ."

The drawing room door opened, and Robert stepped into the hall. "Where the deuce have you been? There has been such a fuss, but I think I have managed to save our necks."

"She knows?" asked Kit.

The footman jumped to open the door to some more guests, and Robert dragged Kit down the hall toward the back stairs.

"No, no, everyone else confessed, but . . ."

"Everyone else? What are you talking about?"

"Claire's secret admirers," whispered the earl. "It seems Northam and Melton were the other two."

"But why . . . how . . ."

"You know my mother. She decided to spread our original idea. If she had only left well enough alone."

Kit grabbed his friend by the lapels of his coat and shook him.

Disengaging Kit's hands, Robert said, "Steady on, Kit. We've nothing to worry about. Claire doesn't suspect us at all."

"So she still thinks she has someone out there sending her love letters?"

"I suppose she must. I certainly did my best to convince her. Make her feel better, you know," said the earl. Frowning, he added, "Still, she'll get over it. The main thing is, she doesn't suspect either of us. I have never seen Claire so furious. She couldn't even speak. I suspect she'll stew over it for a bit and then come down to the ball as happy as a grig, looking for her true secret admirer. Come on. I have guests to greet." Robert walked back toward the front hall, leaving Kit to shake his head in disgust.

He couldn't blame it all on Robert. After all, the idea had sprung from his own wretched mind. And the fact that he had continued to write to Claire . . . he could only suppose his true feelings had been in command.

His hand rested on the smooth wooden post. His eyes

traveled up the dark stairwell while his frown deepened. Claire was upstairs, probably crying, and all because of his stupid idea. The thought was intolerable!

Kit hurried up the stairs, glad he had spent enough time in the Sheffield town home to know which room was Claire's. He paused at the door, listening for her sobs of distress. Silence greeted him, and he wondered if he had the right room.

He lifted the latch and stepped inside.

"Claire?" he said, striding across the room to the bed, sucking in a deep breath when she sat up, apparently quite composed. "Claire, I have to speak to you."

"You needn't bother, Kit. I have already guessed those notes were from you. Do not distress yourself. I know the whole tale."

"You cannot," he said, reaching out to touch her arm.

She flinched and hopped off the bed, moving away from him.

"Look, Claire, there is more to it than you think— more to it than I even realized at first."

"Yes, yes, you'll want to gloat, of course," she said, almost speaking to herself. She forced a pitiable smile and continued, "Very well, Kit. I must admit that I wonder how you managed to keep a straight face when I told you I might be falling in love with my secret admirer. And how you must have laughed at my boasting comments about my admirer's sincerity."

"I didn't laugh at anything. Let me explain, Claire."

"There is nothing to explain," she said, walking past him to sit in the chair beside the fire.

"For heaven's sake, Claire. Rail at me! Claw at me! Tell me to go to the devil, but do not give me this pathetic act!"

"And why not? Is that not how you and all the others see me? Did it never occur to any of you that I would find my own way in London Society? Were you so certain I would fail?"

Heaving a sigh, Kit joined her by the fire, pulling up a footstool and sitting on it, folding his long legs this way and that, and leaning forward to rest his elbows on either side of her lap. He reached into his pocket and pulled out the final letter.

"Just read this. My words are completely inadequate to what I wish to say. I hope this will explain it better."

"What's this?" she said, pursing her lips at the yellow envelope he offered her.

"It was in your wooden box downstairs. I sent it this afternoon, to give you a chance to . . . but you didn't see it, didn't read it."

"Gravely tried to give me something, but I . . . I was too upset."

"Will you read it now?" he asked, his heart in his eyes.

Biting at her lower lip, her hands trembled as she opened the envelope. It was a long letter, not the short verses she was accustomed to. The signature caught her eye first.

She looked up, studying his face, her heart racing.

"You signed it, *Kit,*" she said.

A glimmer of a smile crossed his lips. "That is what one usually does with a confession," he said softly. "Read it."

She nodded, her eyes flying over the page, her expression softening, then growing incredulous.

"You did confess," she said, lowering the paper, wonder in her eyes. "But, Kit, how can I believe the last line? How can I . . ."

"I know. What I did, though motivated by my brotherly affection at first, and then . . . Well, I know you may disbelieve me. And I haven't told you all."

Tears sprang to her eyes at this, and he gathered her into his arms, pulling her onto his lap so he was almost sprawling on the floor.

He took her face in his hands and explained, "I wrote that I have fallen in love with you, my beloved. What I left out was my hope, my dream, that you can love me in return. That you will agree to make me the happiest of men and become my wife."

"Oh, Kit, if you only knew!" she said, throwing her arms around his neck and kissing him inexpertly on the lips.

His chuckle made her raise her head and frown fiercely.

"Are you laughing at me?"

"A little. I was worried all you felt for me was that old childish infatuation. But I see my CeeCee has grown into a woman."

"You knew about that?"

"Always. Young men are frequently dense, but we enjoy adoration."

"You are horrid," she whispered, studying his face for a moment before winding her arms around him again.

Kit gave himself wholly to her kisses, rejoicing that Claire's passion matched his own. When his position on the floor with her on his lap became untenable, he pulled back, settling her more comfortably on his outstretched legs.

"So you will marry me?"

"First things first," she said. "First I will forgive you."

"Agreed. And then you will marry me?"

"Yes, I think I must make an honest man of you, after luring you to my room so you could compromise me."

She started to kiss him again, but he held her back.

"What do you mean by that?"

She smiled, and he scowled in return.

"Do you mean you had guessed I was the writer of those letters, and you were going to use them against me?"

"Now, what does that matter? You love me, and you wish to wed me. What more do you need to know?" she said airily, scrambling off his lap and standing up.

She strolled over to her dressing table and began tucking loose curls back into place.

Groaning, Kit clambered to his feet and followed her. Peering over her shoulder, he studied her reflection in the glass, a suspicious gleam in his eyes.

"Claire, I want the truth. Was all this," he said, sweeping his hand toward the bed where she had lately been curled up like a wounded fawn, "was this all just a ruse to trap me?"

Claire looked at him in the mirror and cocked her head to one side.

"How does it feel to think someone is making a fool of you, Lord Kittridge?"

His black eyes narrowed, and then she smiled.

With a growl, he picked her up and held her, squealing and squirming, until his lips met hers, sealing their bargain and their love.

They heard the door open, but before they could react, two huge paws caught Kit waist high, knocking him off his feet. With a tangle of paws, legs, wet tongues, and rose-colored silk, they collapsed into a heap of laughter.

Kit found the important part and kissed her lips until his efforts were interrupted by Regent's cold, wet nose.

"Argh! Enough! Come here, you long-legged beast. Out you go!" he said, shoving the reluctant puppy out the door, closing it, and turning the key in the lock.

"Now, I have you all to myself," he said.

"Until time for the ball to begin," said Claire, her eyes

lighting with mischief. "We have already missed half of dinner."

"Yes, and it might look a trifle suspicious if we were to go down now, especially since your hair is completely falling down."

"And your coat has two dusty paw prints in the back. You should go to Robert's room and have his valet brush it for you," said Claire, taking a step closer to him.

"And you, my sweet love, should ring for Nellie to come and straighten you out," said Kit, closing the gap until he could take her in his arms again.

Moments later, after crashing into, and then onto, the bed, Kit murmured, "How long until the ball begins?"

"Not long enough," replied Claire with a giggle.

"Hoyden!"

"Cad!"

Another kiss, and then he sat up, tugging at his ruined cravat. He sobered, smiling down at her. "I love you, my dearest CeeCee."

"And I love you, Kit."

He stood up and pulled her to a sitting position, keeping her small hands in his.

"I'll ring for Nellie, shall I? And then I'll go see Robert's valet."

"Yes," she said. "We should be just about presentable by the time the annual Sheffield St. Valentine's Day ball begins."

"Just about," he said, crossing the plush carpet and unlocking the door. Turning, he asked, "Shall we announce our betrothal tonight, my sweet?"

She smiled and nodded.

"I'll be back to escort you to the ball, love."

He opened the door, and Regent bounded inside, planting his feet and looking from one to the other. Claire giggled, and the puppy galloped to the bed, colliding with the corner post and sitting there dazed. He shook his head, gazing up at his mistress, rapt with adoration.

Kit chuckled. "I know just how you feel, old boy, just how you feel."

Then he blew her a kiss and closed the door.

ABOUT THE AUTHOR

Julia Parks lives in Texas with her husband of thirty-two years. She teaches high school French when she is not writing, playing with her grandchildren, or leading a group of students to Europe.

Julia's novels include *The Devil and Miss Webster, His Saving Grace*, and *A Gift for a Rogue*. Be watching for her next novella in the 2003 Mother's Day Regency Anthology. If you would like to contact her, please write to the publisher or send her an e-mail at dendonbell@netscape.net.

VALENTINE DREAMS

Donna Simpson

One

"Hart, you're brooding again. What's wrong?"

Lord Hartley Kentigern glanced up at his sister, Lady Charmian St. Edwards, and shook his head. "You're mistaken, Charm. I'm not brooding. I was just considering . . . the crop in the east field this year."

His sister, a tidy, slim woman of thirty-one years, two years younger than her brother, sat in a chair opposite him, folded her hands on her lap, and stared into his eyes. He turned his face away. "So that is why you are sitting alone in your library of a winter's eve, staring into the fireplace. You are thinking of crops."

"Yes."

"I don't believe you."

"That is not my concern."

Charmian expressed her frustration with a clicking noise and a shake of her head. But the earl refused to elaborate, nor would he let her anxiety on his behalf draw him out. She would worry over him like a ewe over a lamb if he would let her, but he would not have her peace cut up for his sake. As much as he appreciated her desire for his comfort, his thoughts—and his dreams—were his own.

His dreams. He buried his face in his hands and rubbed his eyes, wondering when he would sleep again without that dream. A woman's voice, a woman's delicate touch, her scent, lilacs in rain—it was driving him to distraction and haunting him. He would admit it to himself, if not to his sister. It was just that there was something familiar in her touch, and yet *not* familiar. He couldn't even explain it to himself, and he knew if he voiced it, it would sound absurd.

He had pondered over every woman he had been with in the last ten years—the list was not overlong, but there were a few willing widows and even one divorced woman—but not a one smelled just *so,* or felt just *so* in his arms, as the woman in his dreams. It was beginning to haunt his waking hours, this obsession with figuring out who she was.

Because she touched not just his hair and his body, but also his face. His fingers traced his right jaw and up the right cheek, touching, probing . . . wondering. She touched his face. Caressed his scars.

Why? What did it mean?

Charmian gazed steadily at her brother, waiting for a response to her last statement, which had just been that it *was* her concern, if he was not eating and likely not sleeping. But he hadn't even heard her. He was staring into the fire again; but as she watched him, he raised one hand and lightly touched his face, the scars on his right side a haunting reminder of tragedy, a harrowing night that lived in her own memory as a grim nightmare. She still awoke sometimes thinking she smelled smoke, her heart pounding, her ears ringing, and again she was nineteen and in London for the Season, having a wonderful time until the night that changed her and her brother's life forever, the night of the fire.

The fire.

It seemed so long ago now, and yet sometimes it came back to her with such clarity it was as if it had occurred just the day before. Her father, the Earl of

Kentigern, had been in London with his whole family: his wife, Lady Kentigern; Hartley, who was his oldest son and heir to the earldom; herself, the only daughter of the house; and . . . Lawrence. Little Lawrence, forever seven, her beloved brother, a sweet, energetic, mischievous boy.

Had he been playing with a candle or had the candle just tipped over? No one would ever know how it had started, but it had been conjectured that a candle had caught on a curtain in Lawrence's room on the third floor. Charmian's mother later said her husband had smelled smoke and had raced to his youngest son's room, even as he commanded Hartley to get Charmian and their mother out of the house.

She had huddled with her mother on the pavement outside as the eerie glow of fire in the upper floors and the steady stream of panicking servants had filled the dark night with confusion. Nanny, who had been down in the kitchen getting Master Lawrence a drink of milk when the fire started, stood out on the street, milk still in hand, and set up a high keening wail Charmian could still hear sometimes, ringing in her ears. And she could still remember seeing a dark figure moving by the window of Lawrence's room as the heat shattered the glass with a pop and a tinkle.

Hartley had then dashed toward the house, even as the butler, an older man named Bacon, had pleaded with him not to go, saying that the whole third floor was being consumed. He had tried to get to Lord Kentigern and young Lawrence, Bacon said, but the flames had buffeted him back.

But Hart was not one to listen, and he raced back into the house. He spoke little about what happened next, had never divulged every minute of his sad quest. Charmian had begged to know more, but he was unable at first to find words for the horror of it, and then had said it was too sad and too awful to speak of, especially to her; she had already suffered so much. But she had gleaned he had been unable to get past the flames to his father and brother, though he had heard them. He had heard their shrieks of pain and it still, she thought, haunted him to this day, that he had been able to hear but not help.

Their father and little brother had died that day, and she thought their mother's heart had been buried with them, because she died two years later to the day of the fire, broken and devastated by the death of her husband, whom she loved, and the miracle child, the son she had never expected to have after several miscarriages, and upon whom she had doted.

And Hart was left to soldier on, his face horribly disfigured at first, the burns on the right side of his cheek and neck painful evidence of how hard he had tried to save his father and brother even after all hope was gone. His recovery had been slow; there were burns on his right shoulder and arm, too, and there was some fear at first that he would lose the use of his arm, or that the sores would become poisoned and so his blood.

But assiduous care by an excellent nurse—their old nanny, having lost little Lawrence, would let no one else care for Hart—had proved efficacious, and he had recovered. She was thankful for his sake that he was still able to use both arms and hands. He had lost none of his physical abilities.

But he had lost something more precious to him. He had lost Melony Farramond, his fiancée. Shortly after the fire, she had written him a stiff little note that she was sorry, but she felt they would not suit, and she was breaking off the engagement. She left London that same day, allowing no further contact.

After that day and for many years Charmian had despised her with a hatred so vitriolic it had burned her stomach like acid. Shallow, vapid, selfish; she had damned Melony Farramond with all those words and many more vile ones. She had wished dark and foul fates upon the girl's head. The hatred ate her up for a while, but she had conquered it to some extent, battling it down to merely despising Miss Farramond. Now even that scorn was gone, replaced by some small measure of understanding.

Charmian glanced up at Hartley again. He had sat back in the chair, his face in the shadows, his usual position. What would have happened if Melony had not deserted him as she did? Would he have healed faster? Would his personality not have taken on the dour cast which shadowed it now?

Who could say?

Maybe it was time to find out if old wounds could heal, or if reopening them would just bring further heartache. Maybe it truly was time to take a chance at hurting her beloved brother even more deeply in the effort to heal him of his spiritual wounds, so much deeper than mere burns.

TWO

Miss Melony Farramond, spinster, looked over her mail, and when she found it held the letter she had waited for, she stared down at it, trembling.

Sir Harold Farramond, her father, wandered into the comfortable sitting room and glanced around, his pale eyes glaring into every corner and scanning every surface. "Where the devil are my glasses? Melly, have you seen my glasses?"

"On the table in the library, Father," she said, concealing the tremor of her voice and shuffling the letter in among the others.

"Ever since your mother has been gone, I can't find anything in this blasted household. Your mother would have known where my glasses are."

"On the table in the library, Father," Melony repeated patiently, clutching the pile of letters to her ample bosom and waiting while he turned and shuffled out. He had not been the same since his wife's death just before All Saint's Day of the previous year, three months ago now. As the winter progressed, he seemed older and grayer with each passing day. She was encouraging him to go to visit her younger brother and his wife, who lived on another of the Farramond family properties, a farm near Polperro, but he seemed incapable of making his mind up about anything.

As he exited the room, she found the letter again among the other mail and took it over to the window, which looked out on the dull January scene of withered gray and drab countryside. The Farramond residence was two miles in from the Cornish shore, but the salt wind still blew that far inland, flattening the long grasses left at the end of the last autumn.

Sitting on a hard chair by a polished oak table, she stared down at the letter, wondering if she dared open it. She turned it over and over, tracing the address, noting the texture of the fine linen paper, touching the wax seal. It held an answer, she supposed, but what answer? And even if it held an affirmative, did she dare take the chance and do what she had proposed in a moment of boldness?

Because she was not bold. Life and her family had made her timid, she supposed, though there was no excuse for some of her past actions. She had long come to regret her behavior in many instances.

Especially one. The one she would correct if she could, finally confront if she could not. She touched the blue seal on the letter, tracing the heraldic elements, the stag rampant, the crossed swords. The Kentigern seal.

She laid the letter down on the table, though, unwilling or unable to break that seal yet. She stood and paced away from the table toward the empty fireplace, looking over her shoulder at the letter, wondering if she had done the right thing.

The sitting room was cold and gloomy and she shivered, rubbing her wool-clad arms briskly, but the habits of years would not be broken. No fires in the morning in the sitting room or parlors. No beeswax candles unless company was expected.

Even though her mother had been dead almost three months, the servants would not change their ways, and

Melony had been unable to persuade them to after over
thirty years of stringent thrift. It was not that there was
no money for commonplace comforts; it was just that
things had never been done in such a way, and likely
never would, now.

Her father was of no use, for he merely said Margaret
had had a reason for doing things the way she had, so
they would continue to be done that way. Melony was
nominally the female head of the household now, but
the ghost of Lady Farramond was still the true power in
their home. So the fireplace held only ashes, though in
her mother's lifetime a maid would have already dis-
posed of those. The servants did only the minimum of
work now, knowing Melony was not hard-hearted
enough to dismiss anyone who slacked and was too in-
decisive to enforce the rules. The legacy of her youth
and the tragedy she had witnessed and been a part of
was that she wanted everyone, down to the lowliest
scullery maid, to be happy.

Melony paced back to the window and rubbed her
arms again; she should have brought her shawl downstairs with her. Sometimes she wished she had the
decisive nature of her mother. Lady Farramond never
had wondered if she had done the right thing, nor had
she ever agonized over a decision. And she had deci-
siveness enough for her whole family.

Which was sometimes the problem.

Taking a deep breath, Melony sat. This was ridiculous. She would open the letter and read it. She broke
the seal and unfolded the sheet. What would Lady
Charmian St. Edwards say?

Charmian paused before the door and bit her lip. It
was February first. The last few weeks had seen her take

actions she was hiding from her brother, and she was not accustomed to such subterfuge. But she felt there was no alternative. Given a choice, he would likely not face what she would have him face.

And yet no matter how she justified it, she knew she was interfering in his life. But it was for his own good. She repeated that out loud. "It is for his own good."

With a sharp nod, she took a deep breath and pushed open the door. "I've written a note to the Stauntons, Hart," Charmian said, entering once again his lair, his library.

"Mhmm?"

He was sitting by the crackling fire with his feet up, reading an agricultural paper presented by a friend of his; she knew he had not even heard her. When absorbed in business, his mind was totally engaged.

However—

"Yes," she said, trailing her hand along the table that held a globe, a stack of newspapers, an inkwell, and other writing detritus. Her brother's library was a comfortable room of dark wood bookshelves, thick old carpets, and heavy Jacobean furniture, with a deep chair and a settee placed for comfort near the massive fireplace. It was a truly masculine lair, just as her brother was an overtly masculine man, with no time for feminine tenderness or compassion. "I . . . told them we would both be delighted to attend their Valentine masquerade ball, as always. I have been pondering what you should wear. What do you intend to wear?"

He looked up and frowned over at her, rattling and folding the paper. "What are you talking about?"

She repeated what she had been saying as she came to stand on the hearth, warming her legs against the chill of the room.

"I don't know; that's almost two weeks away. I'll

decide the day before, like I always do." His tone was impatient, his manner careless.

"Won't you give me a hint what way you are leaning? That way I could get the costume out and see if it needs cleaning or mending." She spread her hands behind her back, feeling the blaze warm her cold hands. "You could wear that Tudor courtier outfit," she said, hoping it sounded as if she had just thought of it. "You do look dashing in that."

He snorted. "Dashing? Charm, you're laying it on a bit thick. Save your butter for someone who will believe it."

"Hart," she said, lightly, "you may meet the love of your life! You should look your best."

"Sentimental claptrap! Love of my life." He tossed the paper on a table near his elbow and picked up a cigar, bending past his sister and lighting it with a spill of paper lit from the blaze.

She gazed at him, wondering if he knew how many women had actually fallen in love with him, scarred visage and all. Ever since the hideous fire—and subsequent abandonment by his fiancée—he had engaged in only the most superficial of relationships with women, carrying the anguish of his emotional wounds to ridiculous lengths, in her opinion.

But she did know about the women he had bedded. She and her brother lived a solitary life at Kentigern for the most part, and she could not help but be preternaturally aware of his every mood and so sense the subtle changes in him when he had a mistress, or was involved in an affair. But the affairs were always transient. He touched briefly, like a bee sipping flower nectar, and then danced away. He seemed determined never to allow himself to be hurt so deeply again.

But one or two of his conquests had actually cared for

him deeply, falling in love with his innate gentleness, his sterling character, his loving heart. He had broken more hearts than he knew, and she was weary of his self-defeating attitude and dread of committing himself to more than a sexual relationship with a woman. At this point he was merely carrying a grudge, in her opinion, and it was tiresome in the extreme.

This Valentine's eve would see him confront his demons, if she had anything to do with it.

"Charm, what are you staring at me like that for?" He eyed her as he tilted his head back and blew out a steady stream of smoke. "You have the most baleful gleam in your eye!"

She resolutely ignored the cigar. Propriety dictated no man smoke in the presence of a woman, but she was only his sister, after all, as he had told her when up-braided about his lax behavior. "So you won't tell me what costume you will wear?"

"I don't *know* what costume I shall wear! Now leave me be, you plaguey woman," he said, with mock brisk-ness.

She started past him toward the door, but paused and perched on the arm of his chair. "Hart, you know, I think it is high time . . ." She stopped, unwilling to start an argument, the same old one she had had with him many times. She firmly clamped her lips together and stood, touching his curly mop of hair, graying a little at the temples, with her slim fingers. "You should get Landers to trim this before the ball," she said, naming his under-utilized valet.

"Maybe. Or maybe I will let it grow longer and go to the ball as Beast from the old fairy tale."

She withdrew her hand and balled it into a fist, forc-ing herself not to retort. She was not willing to lash out at him about his self-pity right at that moment. "I am going to town on the morrow. If you need anything, let me know." She strode from the room, her anger making her footsteps short and quick.

Left alone, he sighed and passed one callused hand over his face, drawing deeply on his cigar and then tossing the stump into the fire. He settled back deeper into his chair and closed his eyes. He had rightly interpreted her sudden anger and knew it was justified. He did not often allow maudlin grief to overtake him, but he was tired. He had had the dream again the night before, and then had risen and roamed the house for the rest of the night.

Who was she?

Whoever she was, he wanted her, and badly. Her gentle touch had brought contentment and relief, but he had wakened aroused and restless. Maybe it had just been overlong since he had had the comfort of a woman's favors. If that was the case, the Staunton ball was always rich hunting ground. He had long had the feeling that Donald Staunton, his senior by about twenty years but a good and valued friend, made sure his wife invited a few widows and women of less than sterling morality just for his delectation.

Perhaps he was wrong; he would not make of his friend a procurer. But he appreciated the occasional companionship of a woman willing to overlook his physical failings for a brief, mutually satisfying affair. He always knew which one to single out for his needs. He wanted no messy entanglement, no lasting affair, and so he always chose a woman with the same desire for just a fleeting physical liaison, a sweet interlude in humdrum life.

Not like the women who attended the ball clearly looking for a husband. They made him uneasy, because he could sense some were desperate enough to take even a scarred and bitter man as husband, just for his title and wealth. Charmian said he didn't give them a chance, that he had rejected women who genuinely liked him, who could love him, just out of self-pity.

But he didn't believe her, thinking she had a somewhat unrealistically rosy view of her sex. In his experience women were shallow and flighty, affected more by the externals of a fair face and deep purse than any earnest thoughts of worth. Though perhaps that was not fair to her. After all, she was not like that, and there were bound to be more women in the world like Charm, if only one could sort out the wheat from the chaff. His problem, perhaps, was that he did not trust his own perspicacity to do that.

But it was his own life and he would conduct it the way he saw fit, despite her disapproval. She was not one to cast stones. After all, she, too, had loved and lost, and had not made the effort to find another match.

So he would not be bullied by his younger sister into anything he did not feel comfortable with. He would go to the Stauntons' Valentine Ball, and he would perhaps find temporary bliss in the arms of a willing woman.

And Charm would just have to get over her pique.

Three

Charm was done breakfast when Hart, weary and haggard, joined her, sitting beside her at the long oak dining table. Mid-February sun, weak but brilliant, streamed through the diamond-cut window panes and glinted off the crystal chandelier and sparkling goblets.

"Are you all right?" she asked him, pushing her plate away and nodding to the waiting footman, who took it from her.

Hart motioned to another footman and indicated the coffeepot. Irritably, he waved off offers of food. "I'm fine."

"You are not fine. You look like hell."

"Language, Charm!" he barked, glancing at the servants.

"I am at home. I use whatever language I like," she said, mildly.

"One of these days you will let slip an obscenity when the vicar is here and will be forbidden the sanctity of the church."

"Vicar Smythe would only laugh, and you know it," she said, in a teasing tone. "He is used to my fits and starts. You are unusually cross this morning, my dear brother. What has made you so cantankerous?"

He shook his head and drained his coffee cup, holding it out for more of cook's infamously bitter brew. He was not about to divulge that he had been up most of the night after another dream. This time he had been making love to the unknown woman, running his hands over her voluptuous curves, touching skin so soft it felt like a child's cheek. He had awakened fully aroused and convinced no woman but the one in the dream would ever satisfy him.

"I will not accompany you to the Stauntons' Valentine's Eve Ball tonight." His tone was bleak and bitter; he knew it, but was too tired to modify it.

"What?" Charm was abrupt, that one word uttered with dismay.

"I am tired; no one will miss me. Take Ellen," he said, naming her maid, "and give my apologies to the Stauntons. Tell Donald I shall ride over one day next week and visit."

"B-but you have to go, Hart! You have to!"

He looked up from his second cup of coffee at the sharp tone of desperation in her voice. His sister, her pretty face mild most of the time, was taut with tension, her slim form rigid as she leaned toward him. Something was worrying her. He pondered a moment, but could think of nothing she had said in the past few days that would account for her sudden anxiety.

"Why?"

"It . . . would be rude of you not to come." She straightened and looked away, out the window. "Look outside, we have perfect traveling weather, and how often does that happen in February?"

"Tell Donald and Constance I am ill."

"But you're not . . . are you?"

"I am not truly ill, but I have not been sleeping well and I'm tired. I should be poor company."

Charmian's expression softened and she laid one hand over her brother's. She gazed down at it, at his hand and the puckered, shiny scars from that long ago tragedy that trailed up his wrist and disappeared under his shirt sleeve. "Hart, even at your worst, you are better company than anyone I know."

He covered her small hand with his good one and squeezed. "Thank you, my dear, but I just do not feel up to going this year. The Stauntons will understand."

She took a deep breath and bit her lip. Hart watched her, wondering what was going on behind these lovely brown eyes, the color of chocolate. She was hiding something from him. What was it?

"Please, Hart, go for my sake."

"I don't want to," he said, withdrawing his hands and sitting back, waiting for her next move. They played chess together often over the winter; his game was careful and methodical, hers was quick and fiery.

She straightened. "Then if you are not going, I won't go."

Interesting move. Was she serious? She adored the Stauntons' Valentine Ball and had never missed a year. He had missed once when he was down with the ague, and once just after their mother had died, but she had *never* missed. Even in half mourning she had attended, donning a simple gray domino and sitting out the dancing. It was the highlight of the dreary, damp Staffordshire winter for her.

"All right," he said, just to see what she would do.

Tears welled in her eyes and her lip trembled; her anguish was genuine. Was there going to be someone there, someone special? Did she have need of his support for some reason she was not yet willing to divulge? Or would her hand be solicited, and she wanted him there to give his blessing?

He took in a deep breath, a sharp pain assailing his heart at the thought that he might lose his beloved sister.

But the pain was mixed with hope that she would, at last, find the happiness she so richly deserved. He put his arm over her shoulders and gave her a quick hug. "All right. If it means that much to you, I will go."

"Thank you," she whispered and hugged him, burying her face in his neck. "Thank you, Hart. You will not regret it. I promise you that you will not regret this night."

Melony Farramond stood at the edge of the ballroom floor, nervously fingering her brocade silk mask and watching the dancers. Where was Lady Charmian St. Edwards? She would be wearing, she said, a pale rose domino and a mask of pink spangles. Where was she? And would she, in person, be as helpful and kind as she had by mail these last couple of years?

And would Melony be able to resist her persuasiveness? For Lady Charmian wanted her to behave differently than Melony was comfortable with. They had dissimilar ideas, clearly, about what this ball would accomplish.

But Melony had to be grateful, both to Charmian and the Stauntons, who had kindly fallen in with their plans and invited her to stay at their home over the Valentine's Ball and the few days that followed. She had arrived just that morning from her home in Cornwall, and her reception had been both kind and effusive. Over the course of the day, even though her hosts were busy with preparations and more arriving guests, they had both gone out of their way to make sure she was comfortable. She was not sure they were completely aware of who she was and her relation to Lady Charmian St. Edwards and Lord Kentigern, and so she had been deliberately vague, but they had been charming and kind.

And now she was waiting. The ballroom was cleverly
lit to provide enough light that no one would bump into
each other, but there was still an aura of mystery. Gauzy
draperies shrouded windows and doorways and created
alcoves where benches and chairs had been secreted.
The lighting was dim, chandeliers sparkled and glowed,
wall sconces provided pools of light. It was a lover's
ball, to be sure, and Melony uneasily wondered if this
was the best place to accomplish what she wanted to accomplish.

But it was too late to go back now.

Where *was* Lady Charmian St. Edwards?

Hart wearily surveyed the ballroom, the clever way
Constance Staunton had created bowers with potted
shrubberies and gauzy fabric, the pools of romantic candlelight fringed by puddles of darkness. The Staunton's
Valentine Ball was most definitely an adult affair, with it
understood that some couples would be engaged in activities not best conducted in the hard light of the open
ballroom. No actually scandalous goings-on were en-
couraged, but flirting and kissing were expected, and
many an assignation had been made at the Valentine Ball.

He *would* never and *had* never gone beyond the
bounds of decency at their ball, but he had met many a
woman with whom he had later shared a passionate liaison at a local hostelry. That, indeed, had been his
intention this year, to meet a willing woman and spend
a few mutually satisfying days bedding her.

But his objective this night had shifted. If he had
originally thought to find a temporary mistress, he had
lost that desire. One reason was that no woman in the
world would match his dream lover, the soft, plump, ex-
quisitely willing lady of his recent erotically charged

dreams. But more important to him now, he wanted to find out what Charm was in such a taking over. She had been nervous during the whole long carriage ride, but had deflected any questions he had, preferring silence, it seemed, to awkward queries.

He could only think she had met someone at some time and expected him to be at the Staunton ball. He rather hoped so. After the death of her fiancé, Major Albert Lewis, at the peninsular battle of Salamanca, she had found no one to match him. Hart sometimes wondered if she was not looking for a husband because she did not want to leave her brother alone at Kentigern Castle, the family's ancient and formidable pile. Lewis had died so long ago, almost five years now, and she had shown no interest in attending the Season in London, nor even many of the local assemblies through the long winter. Never had he seen even a flicker of interest in her.

Until now.

He surveyed the ballroom, filling rapidly with shepherdesses, medieval knights, Greek serving girls, and highwaymen. Among the frivolous costumes were an assortment of dominoes in black and blue and red. The space was not as large as the ballroom at Kentigern, now long silent since the death of their father and brother, but the Staunton ballroom sufficed to make a comfortable dancing area, with plenty of room for cozy conversations and flirtations, if one was so inclined.

He had greeted Donald Staunton at the door and would make his obeisance to Constance when he found her. That was where Charm had dashed off to the moment they entered, so he knew he would see them together at some point, likely chattering, maybe about his sister's secret.

He watched the company for a few minutes; old

friends greeted each other, some paired off. The dancing had not yet begun, but the musicians were warming up in their space in a room off the ballroom, and the conductor was conferring with Donald Staunton, probably about the order of the dances.

Hart's eye was caught by a lone figure at the edge of the ballroom dance floor. Something about the young lady's stance touched him, some loneliness delineated in her stooped shoulders and clasped hands. She was dressed as a medieval lady, with a long, fitted brocade gown in silver and ice blue silk, the fabric of her half mask matching that of her dress. The pointed sleeves of the gown touched the floor, and a chain belt lay low on her hips, accentuating the flare.

Her figure was plump and buxom, voluptuously curved, not a sharp angle anywhere. When she grew old she would likely be stout, but for now there was a pleasing symmetry in her rounded contours. The low square neckline of her dress showed ample cleavage, milk white skin setting off a crucifix of amber and silver. She had an abundance of chestnut brown hair that rippled down her back, unbound—no one worried about the authenticity of costumes at a masquerade—and gleamed in the low light. She exemplified the ripeness of a full-bodied woman, and his interest was stirred.

When he was a young man, only a slender, willowy figure would do. It was the first thing that had attracted him to Miss Melony Farramond, his fiancée in that long ago Season before he learned what pain there was in the world. As he got older, though, a more substantial woman pleased his eyes and his body, and his amours of late had been buxom.

The woman in his dreams was plump and full-bodied, with soft breasts and rounded arms. His interest was aroused further as the memory of the dream came back.

FamilyCircle

SUBSCRIBER DISCOUNT ORDER CARD

ANNUAL COVER PRICE	YOUR 1-YEAR RATE	YOU SAVE
$29.25	$16.97	OVER 40%

Order Family Circle today and you'll get 15 issues for only $16.97. You'll save over 40% off the annual newsstand rate on the one magazine that gives you creative ideas for crafts, exciting new recipes and expert advice on beauty and health.

☐ **YES!** Please send me 15 issues (one full year) of Family Circle at the low rate of $16.97 and bill me later.

Name

Address

City

State   ZIP

☐ Payment enclosed.   ☐ Bill me later.

Please allow 6-8 weeks for delivery of your first issue. Cover price is $2.50.
Offer good in U.S.A. only.

J3DS344

Visit us at
www.familycircle.com

BUSINESS REPLY MAIL

FIRST-CLASS MAIL   PERMIT NO 48   HARLAN IA

POSTAGE WILL BE PAID BY ADDRESSEE

FamilyCircle

PO BOX 3153
HARLAN IA 51593-2344

The sensual details still haunted him, the scent of her—
rain-drenched lilacs in full bloom—and the touch of her
gentle hands. His dream of the night before had been
more intense, with him finally feeling her under him,
her pleasing body cradling him as he touched her lips
for the first time. But as always, it was dark and he
could not see her, though she was familiar, somehow.

He gazed at the young woman, his vision partially
obscured by his mask, the full-face mask he always favored. Should he approach her, just to talk? He had to
do something to while away the time until he discovered
Charmian's secret, and he would be doing the young
woman a favor, maybe, if she did not know anyone. Perhaps he could introduce her to some of the local folks,
find her a dance partner or two.

What would it hurt?

Four

Melony felt him before she saw him. A masculine form brushed against her back and a husky voice whispered, "Would the noble lady deign to walk with a peasant?"

A thrill raced down her back, chased by a cold chill. Goosebumps stood up on her arms.

It was him, his voice, his scent. It was Hart, and she hadn't expected him yet, had thought she would need to seek him out with Lady Charmian's help. But she would recognize that voice anywhere, even in the murky shadows of this strange ballroom. She swayed on her feet, and felt the hard wall of his chest at her back. She did not dare turn around, didn't really care what he was wearing or what he looked like. She nodded yes to his request.

He bowed and took her arm as she turned. He was dressed as a huntsman from the ancient days, a brown tunic, a leather belt with a jeweled knife in a leather scabbard, and gauntlet gloves. A short tobacco-gold cape was draped over one shoulder in a rakish manner. Her whole body shivered with chills, and she knew she trembled as he tucked her arm in his. Eleven years. It had been eleven years since she had seen him last, had heard that voice, and yet still he was as familiar as her dreams. She could not meet his eyes.

"You are a stranger here," he said.

She nodded, not willing to trust her voice, not sure if she wanted him to recognize her just yet, if he would by voice. It was enough to be in his presence, enough to feel him close, his body radiating waves of warmth. Swift glances at him took in the fact that the slim boy of her memory was gone, replaced by a broad-shouldered, thicker-waisted man.

"Did you come just for the Stauntons' Valentine's Ball?"

She nodded again.

"Do you have a voice, or are you always delightfully silent?"

She nodded, then shook her head.

He chuckled, a warm, rich sound she had only heard in her dreams since that long ago Season, so confused in her memory now, so filled with pain.

"Well, which is it? Are you always silent?"

"No," she said.

"Ah, she speaks, and yet she says nothing, what of that? Oh, speak again, bright angel!" He was guiding her to a more private corner of the ballroom, beyond the chaperon's chairs and shielded by a grove of potted palms. "Do you recognize my paraphrase?"

"Yes." Romeo's speech to the distant Juliet on her balcony. How strangely inappropriate, Melony thought, since all of her and Hart's romantic opportunities were in the past and all the tragic couple's were in the future at the moment of that speech.

"Good. You are literate and familiar with the immortal bard, at least. Unless you are hoaxing me. You wouldn't do that, would you?"

"No," she murmured, glancing around, wondering where he was so expertly guiding her.

It was rare to find a woman so monosyllabic, he

thought, glancing down at her on his arm. He was enjoying trying to draw her out, though, and he wondered if she was one of Donald's guests, invited with his lonely friend Hart in mind. In past years he had explained his reasons for doing that, inviting women he thought might please his friend.

He had, he told Hart, known for a long time his friend never intended to marry. That was unnatural, he said, from the viewpoint of a happily married man. All he wanted for Hart was what he had with his Constance, the perfect harmony of mind and body, the exquisite compatibility of heart and soul.

And so he would invite women, many of them widows, because he was a matchmaker at heart and hated to see any worthy woman without a husband. Too many young women were left childless widows by the war, and Staunton hated tragedy of any kind—such as a young, healthy man without a wife to love. If his friend only found pleasure with them for the hours they shared a bed, then there was nothing he could do about it. But one of these days, Donald said, Hart would succumb. And he wanted to be an instrument of the bachelor's downfall.

Hart guided his current prize to an alcove protected from view of the ballroom by a drift of gauzy material and floral garlands. She pulled back before entering, though.

Too fast; he was moving too quickly, trying to isolate her from the growing crowd and the attendant noise and bustle. He liked a little shyness in a woman, a dash of circumspection. It made conquest all the more delicious. He did not try to convince her just yet, instead allowing them to stay outside the alcove, in a shadowed spot by a large potted palm.

"Are you a friend of Donald Staunton's?"

"No," she said.

She was close to him, her arm still loosely through his. He covertly examined her, enjoying the view of her décolletage, and the way the cross nestled against her bosom. He wished his left hand were gloveless; he would have liked to pick up the cross and examine it, brush his fingers against that milky skin, his hunger for a woman's touch sharpened into ravening by her nearness.

"You are a friend of Constance's, then?" he said, puzzled.

"No," she said.

"No. So you are not a friend of Constance's, nor of Donald's, am I right?"

"Yes."

"You came here with another guest?"

She hesitated, but then said, her voice so soft and throaty he had to lean down to hear her now that the music had started, "No."

Her breath was warm against his neck, and she smelled sweet. He was beginning to enjoy the mystery; it added a piquant sense of adventure to the hunt. "But you know another guest, and are here at that person's request?"

There was no hesitation this time. "Yes."

"Well, thank God," he said. "I was beginning to think you might have just appeared, like the fairy queen of legend."

She was silent.

He turned to face her, looking down on her blue and silver brocade half mask, her hair a soft aureole of waving curls cascading down her back and over her shoulders. He picked up one rich brown tress with his gauntleted hand and kissed a curl. "All I dare to do," he murmured, seeing her eyes widen. She had lovely blue eyes, guileless and shaded by thick lashes; her lips pouted, full and pink like a rose in bloom. *That* the mask revealed, the full lips and rounded chin. But nothing more, not the shape of her cheek nor the contour of her face.

"The code of chivalry," he said indicating her dress. "You deserve a knight, but a simple huntsman will have to do."

"Yes," she whispered.

"Yes. I would like to hear that word again. If I promise to behave like a gentleman, will you enter this pretty bower with me?"

She hesitated, but finally . . . "Yes."

She must be mad, she thought. Hart was flirting in an expert manner he must have learned in the years since their engagement, for he never was so gallant nor so proficient in their Season. He pulled her into the draped alcove. The candlelight of a nearby sconce showed as a pale glow through the gauzy fabric, and appeared as a fairy light. The rich scent of hundreds of flowers and her companion's male musk, a blend of tobacco and starched linen, teased her nostrils and made her heart beat faster.

"This is better," he whispered and kept her close by his side.

The music was muffled by the fabric and sounded far away to Melony. But everything about this night felt unreal. Hart was pursuing her, but with no serious intent, if she could read him right. And if he knew who she was—

She shied from that thought. Time enough for that later. At some point she had decided on a course more closely aligned with what Charmian had suggested, she realized. When or how or why it had happened she would need to examine later, when her heart would stop hammering and her throat would open up.

They were silent for a few minutes. His presence beside her was enough, for now. But she could feel, thrumming through him, a suppressed excitement she could not understand. His hard body almost vibrated at the points where they touched, arm and hip and leg. His breathing was rapid and shallow.

In the dusky shadow, as another tune started, a drifting, lilting waltz, he turned her and gazed down, his dark eyes gleaming. He pulled her into his arms, the feel of them like bands of steel. Slowly, tantalizingly, he lowered his face until his was just an inch from hers, and his eyes drifted closed as his mouth covered hers.

Shocked but only too willing, she put her arms around him and felt the press of his lips, the right side slightly puckered, just a little hard with his old wounds. Unexpectedly, tears started in her eyes, but she released her old sorrow and let the feel of him, the taste of him in this unexpected moment carry her on a wave of euphoria.

His moist mouth moved expertly over hers, even with the annoying obstruction of their masks, drawing on her lip, tasting her with his tongue, delicately, tentatively pushing into her mouth as his grip tightened and his breathing became labored. She felt her body respond, let herself feel his passion. He was lusty, when the boy she remembered from so long ago was cool, calm, courtly.

But this man was harder, more demanding, and she knew the thrill of giving in, of surrendering to his expertise. He teetered on the edge of impropriety—if there could be anything proper about kissing a complete stranger—but did not touch her inappropriately or make her uncomfortable in any way other than pleasantly. There was a delicious misbehavior in the moment that heightened the heated ardor of their kiss.

When he released her mouth, it was just to gasp in another breath and pull her close again, teasing her lips, a rumble like a growl in his chest as he kissed her again and again, finally lowering his mouth to her throat, his hot breath bathing her neck in warmth. His mask was silk-covered, and slid over her skin.

Her senses were overwhelmed, the sharp knife of desire that shuddered through her as shocking as it was enthralling.

If only . . . if only she hadn't been so foolish as a girl. If only she had not been so easily influenced by others, by her mother in particular. If only—

What would it have been like to know this man, to wed him and be taken to his bed and to be loved by him, their love made richer, perhaps, for the tragedy he had suffered?

The tragedy she had deepened by deserting him.

And yet, who knew what their lives would be like now? The past was the past, immutable. To mourn it was a waste of time. Now she must remember what she had come here for, one reason only: to try to repair the old damage she had done and go home at peace with herself.

But she was willing to put that off for a few minutes of wanton bliss, a few bittersweet kisses, stolen time out of her drab and respectable life. He would have gone further, was on his way down her neck to her bosom, but that was a line that she could not allow him to cross.

She pulled away, and he instantly released her. Would he recognize her voice? She would soon find out.

"You do me honor, sir, but you should be more circumspect." Her voice, she knew, was huskier now than at seventeen. Maybe she would get away with this delicious masquerade a while longer. "You should never kiss a lady so passionately if you do not know what you are starting . . . Lord Kentigern."

Five

"I have not told you my name! You . . . know who I am?"

She almost giggled at the puzzlement in his voice. "I do."

"Have we met? I cannot believe I would not recognize a woman as lovely as you."

Melony hesitated. She did not want to tip her hand by giving too much information. Evasion would be best. She would tell him the truth, eventually, but for these few enchanted moments she wanted to be his mystery. For years she had been dutiful daughter, grieving fiancée, upright spinster; tonight, for an hour, she would be an alluring woman of mystique. This was a fantasy moment, a brief respite from dreary reality. The moment she revealed herself, it would all be over and her life would return to its drab normalcy.

Perhaps this extraordinary daring on her part was just the sensual delight of his kisses addling her sensible brain. Or mayhap it was the mask and the costume, the sense of being someone else for this hour, this moment. But whatever it was—"Perhaps we met in our dreams," she said, remembering all the nights she had dreamed of his touch, of his voice.

He drew in a breath, sharply, but did not say anything. He did not take his gaze from her, even as the music changed and a lively country dance started. Another giggling couple, their masks off already, tried to invade the bower, but Hart said, roughly, "Find your own hiding place." They skittered away with alarmed glances at his growled rebuff.

Melony wondered what she had said wrong. He was brooding, his brown eyes, shadowed by his dark brows, visible behind the mask. He had never brooded when she had known him last. He was a sunny, even-tempered young man. The fire had changed that; would he have regained his equilibrium if she had just had the courage to stay with him, the courage to see him through the darkest period of his life?

She touched his arm. "My lord? Did I . . . did I say something wrong?"

"No," he said, his voice husky. He still stared down at her, the weak light that drifted hazily through the gauzy tulle creating shadows and hollows so that only parts of him could be seen, like a quick sketch done by a skillful artist. "No, you did not say anything wrong. Maybe we did meet in dreams." He pulled off his left gauntlet and with his hand bare, reached up and touched her hair. "Soft. Like silk." He wound one curl around his finger.

She couldn't breathe, and her heart felt as if it pounded any harder, he would surely hear it. His fingers released the curl and it sprang back into place. And still their eyes were locked on each other.

Outside the bower, life went on: dancers swirled to the music, couples chattered and flirted, old friendships were renewed. The noise came to them like a hushed murmur, waves on a pebbled Cornish shore. But Melony would not have traded places with any woman, even the happiest in the ballroom, if it meant giving up this moment, this second, as his bare fingers trailed down her neck, calluses scratching her tender skin. She closed her eyes and felt him come closer.

"Tell me your name," he whispered in her ear, his free hand snaking around her back and pulling her close. "You know mine. It is only fair."

"Does my name matter so?"

"No. But I do not believe I have ever kissed a woman before I knew her name."

"Perhaps you do know it and you have just misplaced it in your memory."

"It could be. But tell me again and I promise I will never forget it."

"Mystery adds piquancy to the kisses, do you not think so, my lord?" Saucy words, so unlike her to utter.

He chuckled, and bent his head, kissing her again. "Does it?" he murmured, raising his head. "Mm . . . perhaps. But nonetheless, I would call you something, Miss . . . You are a miss, aren't you? There is no jealous husband I need worry about? No reason for your evasions?"

Stung by his casual tone when talking of such a matter, she said, "I have never been married."

"Really!" He seemed startled by her assertion, and disappointed. "Well, good. I would never dally with another man's woman."

"I honor your morality, my lord. Though you say it much as you might say you would never steal another man's horse."

He laughed, throwing his head back, the sound a harsh bark. "Puss has claws. I like that." Touching her neck again, his hand curling possessively around as he drew her close to him, he gazed down at her, a smile still in his eyes. "What is your name? What may I call you, other than enchanting?"

Her eyes stung with tears, remembering how gentle and sweet he was the year of their courtship. For a girl of seventeen he had been the perfect beau: undemanding—he had only ever kissed her cheek and her hand—gentle, patient . . . until the tragedy, anyway. She sadly turned away from the memories. She knew all of that was over; she just wanted . . . no, *needed* some peace in her mind. Needed to know that he was happy, despite the darkness that had shadowed his life. Lady Charmian's letters had been a lifeline, assuring her he had physically healed from the horrendous fire that took his father and brother, but the letters spoke, too, of a bitter man, hardened into steel by suffering.

And yet tonight—tonight he seemed lighthearted, flirtatious, happy, even. She made him laugh, made him happy. And he kissed her with passion and a lust for the physical that did not indicate a dead soul. Perhaps the resolution she so desperately needed to a difficult period in her life could help him, too. Maybe. Or perhaps the plan would miscarry and she would hurt him all over again. She turned away from that dismal thought.

"Still silent," he chided. "I shall begin to think you do not have a name, that you are a daydream, an illusion, a chimera created by my lonely mind."

Lonely. It hurt to hear him say it. "Are you lonely, sir?" She said it gently, touching his arm.

He tried to laugh, but the sound died. "I was just . . . I didn't mean that."

But he did. A dull pain throbbed in her chest, and she put one hand to her breast. Had she deepened his unhappiness by her callous, unfeeling behavior? Or had he forgotten her? Was his most grievous suffering from those past events beyond her control?

Would he remember her middle name from their

courtship, she wondered? She doubted it. She would take that chance. "Call me Rose," she whispered.

He pulled her close and she looked deep into his eyes, wondering, if she looked hard enough, if she would see the unhappiness in his eyes.

"Rose," he whispered, and kissed her again, murmuring her name again against her lips. "Rose."

"Why are you lonely?" she asked.

"I told you I didn't mean it," he muttered.

"But you are. I understand. I'm . . . I'm often lonely, too."

He was silent for a moment. "You are? Truly? You aren't just saying that to . . . to sympathize?" The last word was ground out.

"No." She swallowed hard. "Did you ever . . . Have you never been married?" She knew the answer.

"No," he said, sharply. "I have never been so fortunate."

"Have you ever been in love?"

He flinched, as if she had probed an infected wound, one that would not heal no matter how much salve was put on it. "I thought I was."

She deserved that bitter retort for asking questions unfairly. He didn't know who she was, and it was wrong to abuse his lack of knowledge. "I have known love, though I have never been married."

"But it did not work out?"

"No. Sometimes things happen."

"Things happen," he echoed. He pulled her back to the carved wood bench at the back of the bower and sat down, indicating the seat beside him. "Do you have anyone who will miss you if you sit here with me and talk?"

"No. I am quite alone here. With you."

He shook his head, his eyes gleaming behind the silk mask. "I can't imagine why you are alone. Nor can I imagine why you are with me."

"Lord Kentigern, you have many qualities that would attract a woman to your side."

"And many more that would repel a lady."

Was he speaking of his physical scars, or his emotional ones? She was seated on his right. He likely did not realize his mask did not cover all the scars on his face; his jaw was puckered and part of his neck. It hurt to see it and to know she had abandoned him before the scars even started to heal. "If there is one thing I have learned in my life," she said, trying to keep the tears from thickening her voice, "it is that none of us is perfect. I have tried to forgive myself for unforgivable things I have done, but it is difficult."

He slewed a glance sideways at her. "You? What unforgivable things could you have ever done? You seem a perfect little turtledove to me." He reached out and caressed her shoulder.

Again, a shiver raced down her back. Did any other woman feel this way when a man who attracted her touched her? Her mother had always said a lady was too delicate to feel such things, but she found herself breathing faster and wishing she was in his arms again. He slid closer, as if in response to her unvoiced desire. His thigh was hard and muscular.

"Do you think me an innocent? I am not a child."

"I am well aware of that. No man who held you in his arms and kissed you could think you a child."

She sighed wistfully. She had thought all feeling for him but compassion and regret dead. But it seemed that there still flickered a tiny flame, maybe an ardent ember. She must tamp it down, though, because it was inappropriate, and the moment she revealed herself, she would have to fight to keep even his regard, such as it was.

She had let herself get carried away this night, when

Donna Simpson

she had meant to just meet him, talk for a moment, and then reveal herself for who she was and demand a private meeting with him. His flirtation had been too alluring, his presence too seductive. She had been caught up in the sweetness of the moment, and now she did not know how to get back from where she was.

How could she tell him the woman he had been flirting with and kissing was the one who destroyed his life?

Hart slid his arm around her again and held her close. Rose; a suitably lovely name for the woman who had captured his interest so wholly. It occurred to him he had quickly forgotten his mission to find out why his sister was so insistent he come this night to the ball, but they were only an hour or so into the ball. It would go on until the early hours of the morning, so there was much time. And if Charm wanted to find him, she could. He just could not tear himself away from the lovely and alluring Rose.

They sat together on the bench at the back of the little bower and did not speak, silence enveloping them like a warm blanket. It was at this once-a-year ball that, masked and costumed, he felt like a normal man, and it always freed him to approach ladies who attracted him, flirting with them, kissing them. This was not unusual behavior for him, and yet it felt different somehow. Rose was different.

She admitted to being lonely, too, though that could just be her subtle way of urging him to hasten his wooing. She was unmarried, most likely an innocent, though that did not always follow. Was she amenable to a quick affair? Had he made plain his sexual interest?

And yet the thought of taking her to the local

hostelry and spending a couple of days making love to her, while enticing, left him feeling chilled. Always after those hasty affairs he felt sated, but lonelier than ever. Charmian had come to understand, and left him alone to recover his normally equable nature in peace. He suspected she knew more about his life than they spoke of.

A few times he had received letters from the woman he had been with asking to meet him again, but he could never bring himself to continue the affair, only to see her lose interest eventually. Or to lose interest himself, which was another fear. A sexual conquest, to his secret shame, often did not mean he cared a jot about the woman as a person, though he was always kind, he hoped, and believed he gave as much pleasure as he took.

Rose shivered.

"We are near an open window," he said, twisting and gazing through the sheer draperies. "Those dancing are probably getting much too warm, and so somebody has opened the window. You should really be sitting beside a fire. Would you like to go somewhere . . . more private?"

She hesitated, and he held his breath; he wanted to do this, wanted to talk more, kiss more. But she claimed never to have been married, making her more innocent than his usual flirts. Or likely more innocent, anyway. If she said no, he would have to give up any hope of a casual affair of the kind he was used to.

Given his thoughts of a few minutes before, did he most want her to say yes, or no?

"I don't think it is quite right," she said, "to desert our kind host and hostess."

Ah, an equivocation. "Donald will neither care, nor will he even notice, and Constance is far too busy to remark on our disappearance. Will you go with me? Trust me?"

She hesitated only a moment before she put her hand in his. "I will," she said, softly. "I will trust you."

Six

Trying not to make it obvious that she was searching for someone, Lady Charmian St. Edwards, apprised of Miss Melony Farramond's blue and silver costume vaguely in the style of a medieval lady, scanned the crowded ballroom. After talking to Constance Staunton, who had nothing but praise for Miss Farramond's demeanor and appearance, she went in search of her brother. She had been looking for him for half an hour without success, and was now looking for Miss Farramond.

As for her own appearance, she was dressed in a costume meant to look like Queen Boadicea, that ancient Briton warrior. It was symbolic, in a way. She was fighting for her brother's life, she felt. He was, over the years, sinking deeper and deeper into a morass of cynicism and self-pity, and she was helpless against his anger and bitterness. He did not let it affect his treatment of his sister; he was ever kind and considerate of her, but he would not allow himself to love. It was as if he could not take such a risk ever again, and yet Charmian knew of many women who had cared for him deeply, and even one who had loved him. A friend of hers had come to visit one summer and had fallen deeply in love with Hart, finding in him a depth of passion and strength and a wounded spirit that moved her, but he had resolutely resisted her considerable charms.

Was it just not a good match? Sometimes love was one sided, and it was no one's fault; she had good reason to know all about that. And yet she did not think that was so in this case. Hart was not open to love, so even if there had been a possibility with her lovely friend, he was so scarred by old pain that it seemed he could not feel. She thought perhaps he feared the pain.

Whatever, she had decided it was time to shock him into facing his grief and either defeat it or . . . She did not want to think of the alternative. Over the years she had raged at him, called him selfish, tried sympathy, relentless hectoring, but nothing had worked to lift him out of his pit of self-hate. Being faced with the woman who had put him there just might shock him out of it, or it was entirely possible that that pit was bottomless and he would sink out of sight and beyond reach.

Or—

Or it could just break his spirit completely. She was taking a chance and she knew it. She was being everything she hated in others by interfering in her brother's life. And yet she was determined.

Where was he? And where was Miss Farramond?

Finally she spotted her brother's brown huntsman costume, but—damn him—he had found a woman, one of the only reasons he came to the Staunton masquerade.

He was accompanied by a woman in a medieval costume. A blue and silver medieval costume.

So they had found each other after all, and without any help. Lady Charmian smiled as she watched him guide Miss Melony Farramond toward the doorway that led to a long hall. Maybe things would turn out all right after all. If her brother and Miss Farramond were going somewhere to talk, then maybe it would all turn out for the best. Giddy with relief, she turned and joined a group of friends, intent on enjoying what remained of the evening.

* * *

She must be out of her mind. Melony felt the cold
rush of the frigid air in the hallway, where couples lingered, talking in hushed tones and flirting, as the doors
to the ballroom closed behind them. She was still shivering, but it was not from the cold. Her heavy brocade
costume was warm enough, compared to some of the
scanty outfits worn by the other ladies, some garbed as
courtesans, others like Oriental harem girls.

She was allowing this under false pretenses, though.
Hart thought he was making a conquest, no doubt. And
she had no idea where he was taking her. He had grown,
in eleven years, from a gentle, considerate boy into a
harder, more aggressive man. His passionate kisses left
little doubt as to his intent.

Would he demand she take off her mask once they
were where they were going? And would he recognize
her? She was sadly changed, she feared, from the slim
child she was at seventeen, having become plump and
thick-waisted with the years.

"In here," Hart said, pushing open a huge oak door,
pulling her into a dim room, and closing it behind them.

She hung back, afraid now that the time was nearing.
He felt her resistance and stopped.

He looked down at her, and something in her eyes
must have touched him. She could see the expression in
his eyes soften, melt. He reached up and twined one curl
around his finger. In that moment she remembered the
gesture from their brief engagement. He was a sensual
man, in the way of being very observant of, and sensi-
tive to, textures and touch. He loved fine fabric, sweet
scents, and had once likened her hair to silk, just as he
had this night.

"Don't be afraid, Rose. I would never harm a woman,

nor would I ever try to convince one against her conscience. If you want, all we will do here is talk."

His voice was gentle; her heart warmed and her fears dissipated. This *was* the man she had known. He still retained the kindly nature beneath the fierce sensuality.

"I am not afraid of you, my lord, but . . ."

"Call me Hart. We are not strangers, you say; then call me by my given name. I want to hear it on your lips." His tone was urgent.

"Hart," she whispered, searching his eyes, trying to find her destiny there.

An intense gleam blazed in their depths and his breathing quickened. He closed the space between them and pulled her close against his solid chest. She laid her head there and listened to the thud-thud-thud of his heart.

"Hart, I am not afraid of you," she murmured. "I could never be afraid of you. You have never hurt anyone in your life."

"How do you know that, my dear?"

"It is not in you. I can feel that; I have no need of proof."

"Come and sit by the fire. Warm your feet."

He guided her through the library—that, she saw, was the room they had entered—and sat her down on a padded sofa facing a gargantuan fireplace with a cheery blaze in it. He poured two crystal glasses of sherry and set them on the table at her side. Then he knelt at her feet and slipped off her slippers, chafing her feet, his one bare hand wandering only a few inches up her leg. She trembled.

He sighed and sat down on the sofa, pulling her feet up onto his lap. "I know I am being overfamiliar. Forgive me, Rose."

"There is nothing to forgive." Nothing she considered

a transgression, anyway, as shocking as this would be construed by some.

"Tell me about yourself."

So he was not going to demand an unmasking right now. Why was that? Was it because he was loath to display his scars? Her heart ached for him, and for the years of anguish he had suffered, losing his father and brother, and then, Lady Charmian said, their mother had died, a broken woman, just two years later.

Why had he never married?

"There is not much to tell."

"Come now, I can tell you have a story, Rose. Tell me some of it, at least, even if you do not want to tell me your full name."

He rubbed her stockinged feet and she was lulled into a profound state of relaxation, something she would never have thought possible, especially with Hart. She should be telling him who she was and why she was there, but the lure of being with him and the desire to continue this sweet, seductive dream overtook her good sense. She had the rest of her life to be sensible and wise; for now she would be foolish and selfish.

"I am twenty-eight and unmarried. I have been engaged twice, but have been . . . unlucky in love."

"An all too common quandary," he murmured.

His fingers trailed up her leg in a slow, tantalizing crawl, and her breathing quickened. "I live with my father, and I don't suppose I shall ever marry now," she said, going on as if he were not doing what he was doing. "My father needs me, and I cannot desert him now that my mother has passed away."

"But you should not give up your life for your father!" he said. He massaged her calf and then moved up to her thigh; his fingers hooked over the top of her garter, touching naked flesh. "Surely even such a close tie as that . . . He would not demand that you give up your life. You are a young woman still. A beautiful young woman."

He had stopped rubbing, and his hand rested lightly on her thigh; she was so aware of just that light touch that she felt suffocated desire. She would never have foreseen this yearning she felt for him still, after all these years. How wrong she had been, at seventeen, to listen to her mother, as well-intentioned as that lady had been; but there was no point in self-recrimination over the past. What was done was done.

"I have made grave mistakes in my life, and now I think I will be content to just do what I think right." Summoning all her willpower, she pushed his hand away, and he withdrew it without any demur. She brushed her skirt down over her legs. "I must make amends where I can," she continued. "Repair the damage I have caused, the hurt I have done."

Hart frowned. He eased a little farther up the sofa so she was almost sitting on his lap, and he snaked his arm around her back. "What harm can you have done? I can feel how gentle you are, how good."

She shook her head. How little he knew. "Sometimes harm is not an active thing, but a passive. You can harm someone by allowing others to persuade you to inaction, or to wrong action. You can hurt someone just by doing nothing, when you should be doing something. Sometimes you can cause grave injury just because you are too young or too selfish, too hesitant or too stupid."

"And are those things you have done or been?"

She nodded and covered his bare hand with her own. "I have. I was young once, and afraid. I let fear convince me that what I was doing was right, when in my heart I knew it was wrong."

"You made a mistake. There is nothing shameful in that."

"There is if the mistake you made does something horrible, changes someone's life."

She sounded so very sad. Hart stared off into the fire, his gaze tracing the ancient lines of the baroque carving as he thought of her words, and how it applied to his own life. If he had not hesitated before running back into the blaze, would his brother and father be alive even now? His hand went up to his face, and he felt the puckered edge of his scars, the badge of his failure, at the edge of his face mask.

Failure. What a bitter word.

"I understand," he whispered, not trusting his full voice. He took her hand in his own and they sat for a while, just watching the fire crackle, an ember popping; a log tumbled in the grate. Her hand in his, her body close to him, he felt more connected with his mysterious Rose than he had with any of the women he had made love with in eleven years. They had both loved and lost, and felt the weight of failure loom over them. It was like she knew him, could feel his sorrow, shared his loneliness.

And it frightened him badly.

Seven

It frightened him because of the warmth of his feelings toward her, stranger though she was.

Was it possible? Could he have found a woman who would love him, accept him just as he was? As the silence lengthened, he watched her eyes. It was all he could see of her, other than a bit of her lips and chin. She could be hideous, for all he cared. In the past, his conquests had been known to him by reputation as beautiful women before ever he bid one take off her mask. But this time he knew nothing about this young woman but what she had told him, which was precious little.

And yet in an odd way he felt he knew her better than even his own sister. Rose felt some of his pain, his regret. Whatever she had done—or not done—she was as pained by her failings as he was by his own.

"Kiss me, Rose," he whispered, and drew her close, cradling her in his arms. Their lips met, and it was with new hope that he kissed her, a new blooming of fear and rapture mixed. Her soft mask was in his way, and he began to feel maybe it was time to reveal the real him. It was always difficult, that moment, and he always prepared his inamoratas, warning them of his scars, waiting for the rejection that occasionally came.

He trailed his bare fingers down her neck and touched the delicate skin of her bosom, fingering the amber and silver cross and feeling the enticing dip of her deep cleavage. Hunger burned in the pit of his belly, and as she shivered at his touch, he wondered if she could feel his arousal.

"Rose, I have to tell you a little about myself, though for a woman you have been strangely incurious. Is that because . . . you know something about me? You know my name, so I must assume that we have met, or . . ."

She hesitated, and he wondered if she had learned to distrust herself early in life, and now feared doing or saying anything wrong, making a commitment to words or deeds because of her own failings. He could sympathize with that.

"I know . . . some about you, but not much. Our acquaintance was many years ago. I have since asked questions of one who knows you well."

"Then . . ." He took a deep breath. "You know my face is scarred?"

She nodded, and her lovely eyes welled with tears. Normally impatient with pity, he touched the tear behind the mask and said, softly, "Don't cry for me, Rose. If you already know the worst, I am beginning to think maybe there is hope for me, scarred and bitter as I have been."

"You . . . you don't understand. I am not crying for *you*. You lived, after all! I am crying for the ones who died, for . . . for little Lawrence. And Lord Kentigern, a noble and kindhearted man."

His stomach twisted and burning tears started in his own eyes as his bitter failure came back to haunt him. "If only I had tried harder, been faster . . ."

"No, Hart, there is not a thing you could have done differently. I know that."

"How do you know?" he whispered, his voice choked.

It was time. Melony knew it and yet she could not move, could not take the action that would change the whole texture of their brief, tenuous connection. Somewhere a clock ticked, a mechanism clicked into place with a deep "thunk" of gears, and then the timepiece bonged, the chime sounding repeatedly in the hushed silence of the library.

Twelve. It was midnight, the witching hour, and now Valentine's Day, a day for lovers. But for her it was the unveiling hour. Time to turn back into the cinder girl from an enchanted princess.

"I know." She shifted, moving away from him and straightening her gown with impatient hands. "I know, Hart. I know all about your pain, your sacrifice. I know how you have blamed yourself these years, though nothing was your fault. And I know about the callow, vicious girl who deserted you."

"No," he whispered.

She turned back to him and was shocked at the terror in his eyes, the stark horror. Was he even now beginning to understand, coming to realize who she was? And yet, she must have time, must make her amends, do what she came to do. "She was painfully foolish, Hart, and has long regretted her action. Her only defense is that she was young, and was persuaded to desert you by those who seemed to have her best interests at heart. Indeed, those who *did* have her best interests at heart, but did not know how her best interest could only be served by real love and patience and time."

He frowned behind the mask, his mouth twisted into a grimace. "Who are you? Why have you come here?" he whispered, his voice harsh and grating, raw with pent-up emotion. He reached up and tugged at the strings of her mask, tied behind her head.

She grasped his hand. "I'll do it."

Taking a deep breath, she pulled at the simple knot that tied the silk cord and the bow came loose. She pulled off the mask and gazed at Hart without the obstruction. And without the self-delusion, she realized, once she saw the bitter fury in his eyes. He felt used, hoaxed, she knew suddenly. He didn't understand why she had come masked, why she had allowed the masquerade to continue for so long. She had to explain, had to make him see that it was intended as no joke or painful slight, but merely a way to get to see him. She opened her mouth to speak, but he rose in one swift motion and stood, tall and straight.

Without a single word, he turned on his heel and strode out, slamming the door behind him and leaving her alone in the dusky depths of the library to weep, knowing it was useless to follow.

Lady Charmian St. Edwards could hardly conceal her delight. Every dance she danced was done with a quick and eager step, every conversation seemed brilliant and funny. Dancing with her host and friend, Donald Staunton, she chuckled at some mild witticism of his and then glanced around the room. "I think this is the most magnificent Valentine's Ball you and Constance have ever held," she said. "The house looks magnificent, as do the hosts!"

"And I think you are fairy-charmed, my dear child," he said, indulgently. "I know you and Connie have been up to something; what is it and why has it made you so buoyant?"

She eyed him complacently. "I have a feeling that things are going to be very different for Hart from this day forward."

Staunton's expression grew more serious. "Charm, what have you done?"

They were parted by the figures of the dance, and she considered her answer. Should she tell him now? There could be no any harm in it. As dear, close friends, the Stauntons knew all about Melony Farramond and the debacle of her desertion of Hart. They had agreed with her many years before that her brother had never put the terrible conclusion of his engagement behind him.

But she had still been unsure of how they—especially Donald—would view her interference. Constance she had had to confide in, and the older woman agreed it was time Hart faced his past. Now, having seen Hart and Melony going off to have a private word, Charmian had gained confidence that she had done the right thing. Her beloved brother would talk to Melony, they would settle their differences, and he could finally put an end to his years of bitterness, and maybe even find a wife among the many women who still found him desirable, and even handsome, scars and all.

"I have done the right thing." She told him about her plan to bring Hart together with his former fiancée, forcing them to hash out the past and maybe even forgive and forget the old hurts. Though the pain was all on Hart's side, she had always felt, and the offense on Melony Farramond's.

As the music ended and Donald Staunton returned her to his wife's side, he looked grave and doubtful. "Charm, are you sure this was right? I have misgivings, *grave* misgivings . . ."

At that moment a liveried servant approached them and bowed, then turned to Charmian. "My lady," he said, and held out a silver salver. "My Lord Kentigern asked me to give you this note."

She frowned, and glanced around. "Where is he? Has the naughty fellow gone off with Miss Farramond?"

The servant remained silent, and Charm unfolded the note. She trembled.

"What is it?" Donald Staunton asked, his wife clutching his arm in sudden fear.

Tears starting in her eyes, Charmian shook her head. "He has taken a horse from your stable and ridden home, leaving me the carriage. He says . . . he says he can't stay another minute in the same house as . . . as that woman."

"He means Miss Farramond," Constance said, faintly.

Charmian nodded, and the tears flooded her brown eyes, spilling out and down her cheek, emerging from under her pink spangled mask. "What have I done?"

Eight

Two days of stony silence were all Charmian could stand. She wrung her hands together and stood outside of Hart's library, undecided, and yet knowing she had to do something to repair the damage she had unwittingly done. Again, she had already taken a step and would do more, but it was in the nature of a desperate act now, and not with any real hope that it would solve things. For all she knew the situation, as bad as it was, could get worse. But she couldn't do *anything* if he would not talk to her.

She abruptly pushed open the door and strode in but then stopped, bleakly staring at her brother, sitting by the fireless grate, his head in his hands in a position of abject misery. Her heart spasmed in shared pain. She crossed the floor and knelt by him.

"Hart, please forgive me. I thought I was doing the right thing."

"How could you think that?" His voice was muffled.

"It's been eleven years! Hart, I thought if you could just meet face to face, you would get over it, could move forward with your life instead of remaining mired in the past."

"What do you know?"

She stood. "I know what it is like to lose someone I loved." Damn him and his self-pity! Angry, she paced to the window and glared out at the frosted landscape. Clamping down on her lip didn't help. She was still just as angry. She whirled. "For God's sake, Hart, she was seventeen! A child! Your wounds were raw and ugly, and she was frightened."

"I know that," he said wearily, raising his face. Sunlight touched the puckered edge of the scars and he closed his eyes. "But I can't forgive it. I just can't. She had promised to love me forever. Should have known it was all just words, but I was a sentimental fool at two-and-twenty. But even then, if she had met me as an adult and an equal after all these years I could have forgiven her, but instead she hoaxed me, made a fool of me by pretending to be interested in me. I thought . . ." He groaned and buried his face in his hands again.

Charmian returned to his side and knelt by him. "What did you think, Hart? What?"

He couldn't say it. Couldn't confess that just for a moment, before she revealed herself, he thought he might have found a woman to love again, to care for and who could care for him. Fool! He didn't believe in love. All sentimental claptrap, as he was fond of saying. He stayed silent.

"She said she was not going to do that. She said she would not continue the charade after the first few minutes, that she wanted to confess who she was almost immediately so she could talk to you."

"I knew you did not put her up to it. It was all her own selfish plan." He missed the guilty expression on his sister's face as he still stared into the empty grate. "When did she write to you? Did she suggest this immediately, or deceive you in some way with some false story?"

Charmian hesitated. She sat down on a low stool near her brother. "Hart, look at me!" When his gaze was turned her way, she continued. "Please know that what

I have done, I did because I was worried for you." She
looked off toward the window and took in a deep breath.
"It was I who first wrote to her."

"You *what?*"

He almost stood, but she put a restraining hand on his
knee. "Listen! I wrote her a letter—it was very nasty, really—telling her how badly she had hurt you and
blaming her for everything."

He slumped back down in his chair. "Charm, you
didn't!"

She shrugged. "I was angry and sick of your self-pity,
if you want to know the whole truth. And it was all her
fault! I needed just to say it and be done, at long last.
This was, oh, three or four years ago."

"That long ago?"

She nodded, silently. "She wrote back. Said she understood how I felt, that she had long been sorry for
what she did and how she did it. She didn't make any
excuses, just asked how she could make amends. I told
her she couldn't, that the past is the past."

"And so how did *this* sorry escapade come about?"
he said, his tone harsh and his eyes blazing with hurt.

She winced, but carried on, determined to make him
see why she had done it. "Lately, you have been . . ."

He waited, but then supplied, "Moody? Bitter? Ab-
stracted?"

She met his gaze. "All of those things. And desolate
and dreary and desperately miserable."

"Did you ever think I might have some private, current reason for my moods?"

"No," she said. "I thought it was the old pain. Was I
wrong?"

He frowned. "Yes and no. I don't know. To be truthful, I am bloody sick of myself just now. To see myself
through your eyes is to see a man who has contributed

most of all to his own unhappiness. Unforgivably self-serving and tiresome. Go on."

"So I thought about what Miss Farramond—Melony—said, that she wanted, just once, to talk to you again, to see you and say she was sorry. She really is sorry, Hart."

"If that was so, then why the charade? Why not just invite her here and let her say her piece?"

"I cannot explain why she did not reveal herself to you immediately; you would need to ask her that yourself." She took a deep breath. "I was the one who suggested the charade, as you call it. I thought if you two could talk without you going all harsh and silent that you might break the ice, so to speak. The ice being your crusty old heart." She touched him affectionately on the shoulder, but he moved away irritably.

Sighing, Charmian went on. "I just know what she intended. She didn't want to come *here,* which is why I thought of Donald and Constance's home. And the only time I could depend upon you being there was the Valentine's Eve Ball. The timing was just right. She thought it would be unfair to come here, to invade your home and leave you with no recourse but to be polite to her, as your guest."

He gave a harsh bark of laughter and smacked the arm of the chair. "How little she knows me, after all. I wouldn't have had any trouble being rude to her, even on my own property. *Especially* on my own property."

"Hart, that is enough," Charmian said, standing. "You have it all wrong. For years, I think, you have been virtually blaming her for the fire itself, so confused and labyrinthine have become your feelings. I know you. You are kind. *And* gentle. Except where Melony is concerned, and there you are harsh beyond reason. I want you to talk to her."

"I have nothing to say to her," he said. He saw the impatient look on her face, and said, "Charm, I mean it. Even if we came to some understanding, what good would it do? Just to calm her guilt? The past is dead, and there is nothing in the present or future for us."

She moved to stand over him. "If you can tell me honestly that at the ball, before you knew who she was, there was nothing between you, then I will go away and leave you alone, never to mention her name again."

He was silent for a moment, but then growled, "That was an illusion. I thought she was someone else."

"But there was *something.*"

"I . . ." His face shadowed with old pain, he nodded. "I thought there was something there, and for a fleeting moment I thought it was mutual."

"Perhaps it was. She has matured, Hart, grown up—and so have you. You are different people now."

He shook his head. "If she is unmarried still, it just means that perhaps she can now swallow her repugnance at my scars to capture my title and wealth. I was masked. It likely helped."

Charmian made a noise of disgust in her throat. "Lord, but you are self-pitying! Do you know how annoying you have become, and how whining?"

He glared at her. "Did I ask for your opinion?"

"You need to resolve this with Melony. Trust me, Hart, I have hated her for what she did to you, but now I think I understand. Talk to her."

"No."

"Yes." Charmian strode to the doorway and exited, returning one minute later. "Talk!"

She shoved someone ahead of her and closed the door of the study. Hart heard a latch click, and realized his darling younger sister had locked him into the room with . . . with Miss Melony Farramond, unmasked, and

even lovelier than he had dreamed. Her rounded figure
was draped in a soft blue day gown of some clingy fabric, but he determinedly lifted his gaze to her face.

She looked frightened, standing just inside the door,
her hands behind her, her eyes wide and fixed on his
face.

His face.

"Get out," he grunted, as he turned away and slumped
down into a chair.

There was silence. He covered his face with his
hands. "It is not a much prettier sight now than it was
eleven years ago," he said. "Hammer on the door and
demand my idiotic sister let you out. How she convinced you to come here, I do not know."

"I asked if I could."

He stilled, his whole body rigid as her voice, so gentle and husky, brought back the delirium that had seized
him two nights before at the Staunton ball. He felt again
her luscious form cradled against him and the taste of
her sweet lips. He felt again the horror when he realized
what he had been tricked into.

"It was a despicable act," he said. "How could you do
it? How could you kiss me? Knowing . . ." He shook his
head and looked up, daring to meet her gaze, waiting for
the disgust. "Knowing."

She took a step forward. "Knowing?"

"Knowing . . . the scars, the past. Knowing all of it."

Melony gazed at him, staring at the scars that marred
one side of his handsome face. His cheek and the side
of his eye, right down to his chin on the ride side, all of
the skin was wrinkled into random crisscrosses that
looked like roads on a map. "It didn't seem to matter,"
she said, simply, moving forward another step. "Lady
Charmian has locked us in here because she would have
us resolve our differences."

He stood, and she realized again how changed he was from the slim, vigorous young man he had been. He was broader, more powerful, his thighs as thick as tree trunks and his torso broad, even at the waist, once as narrow as a girl's.

But she liked the changes. She had changed, too, after all. It was what had led her to put off the moment of revelation. Being held in his arms had been an awakening. She had come merely to put the past to rest so that she could go on with her life, such as it was, with no regrets. The years under her mother's governance had taught her that the woman she had thought at seventeen knew everything had been flawed, snobbish, and hard, but had nonetheless thought she was doing the right thing by guiding her young daughter away from the tragic Kentigern legacy.

"If you want to leave, I will break down the door," he said, his tone steely and bleak.

She shivered. He had been so gentle as a youth. Was he now irredeemably hardened? Charmian said no, and Melony had proof he could be gentle; the way he touched her and kissed her at the ball had not been the actions of an irredeemably harsh man.

"There is no need to break down the door on my behalf, my lord. I am content to remain here. But your sister is rather dramatic. She did not need to lock the door."

"She locked it not for your sake, but because she knows I am prone to hasty decisions."

Melony crossed the floor and noted, as she did so, his movement. He stepped back, as if to move away into the shadows, and then must have decided to stand his ground and moved forward again. His head went up and his eyes glittered strangely.

"It has been eleven years," she said. "Much has happened in my life in that time, and I would imagine the same is true of you. Can we at least talk, Hart? May I still call you Hart, as I did when we became engaged and as you asked me to two nights ago?"

"I am Kentigern now." His tone was hard.

She nodded. "Lord Kentigern, then," she said, softly, then frowned and shook her head. She moved toward the window and stared out at the bleak landscape. It had rained and then frozen, so everything glittered with a coating of ice. Cold and hard, like the man behind her. "I remember that most of all from the first day, when I came to see you after the . . . after the fire. The servant said Lord Kentigern was resting and could not be disturbed. I . . . I thought for a moment they had f-found your father alive, until I realized that you were the new earl."

"Have you been here since the night of the Staunton ball?"

He did not want to explore old hurts, his change of subject told her.

"No, I came yesterday. I cannot return to Cornwall without explaining my actions."

"I can't think of a single explanation that makes any sense," he said, his tone bitter and weary.

She turned back to look at him again and shrugged helplessly. "I know it seems absurd. When I first heard your voice behind me at the ball, I just wanted to talk to you, to know you were all right. I was afraid the moment I told you who I was you would walk away from me."

"Your fear was justified. I have nothing to say to you, and even less now that you have seen fit to trick me."

"Are you happy?"

"What has that to do with anything?"

"It has everything to do with *you!* I want you to be happy, want you to be able to go on and be happy, to find . . . love."

"Sentimental claptrap! I do not believe in love."

She turned away to the window again. Now that she had him in her power, what to say to him? How to make him understand that though she was sorry for her actions in the past, she could not now change them.

Well, of course he must realize that, but—

"Hart," she whispered, turning back once more to see that he had melted into the shadows by a tall bookshelf. "Hart, do you remember?"

Nine

"Do I remember what?"

She took a step toward him. "Do you remember that spring?"

"I could hardly forget it. I lost my father and my little brother and became *this!* Before you deserted me like a coward."

She held her ground, taking a deep breath. Charmian had warned her, and she would not let his anger and bitterness turn her away. "I mean before that, Hart. Before the pain and horror." She wanted to search for words, but what to say? How to appeal to the man he was before it all?

He turned and moved to the window, one fist resting on the pane as if he was about to break through and climb out. "I don't remember anything before that night."

He was lying. She took one more step toward him. "Yes, you do. Remember . . ." She took in a deep, shaky breath. "Remember the night we first met? It was at the Saunders's ball; they had a theme of An Enchanted Forest, and there were potted trees and whole garden boxes. I saw you first. You were with friends and I heard your laughter before I saw your face. You laughed all the time."

"I was bosky," he said, his tone wry.

"Were you?" She chuckled, folding her arms and taking another step toward him. "That explains much. I was so young, I wouldn't have recognized the signs, I suppose. My father does not drink. I was just caught up in the romanticism of it. You approached me and whispered you had never before believed in love at first sight, but had now to admit it was possible to fall in love on first view of a young lady."

"What a cad I was," he said.

"You didn't mean it, then," she whispered, the laughter dying. Had it all been a lie? How different things looked through the dusky glass of years.

"No. I didn't mean a word of it."

"But you begged an introduction, and asked me to dance. And you came to call the next day," she said, wistfully. "You were very gallant."

"You were the diamond that year. A gentleman of my stature was expected to pay attention to the most beautiful belles."

So he was intent on dashing every fond memory of that spring, squashing it with cold facts and hard truth. She would not let him. "Say what you will, Hart, I fell in love with you. And you soon stopped visiting other girls, paying all your attention to me, and then, that lovely spring day . . ."

She stared at the window and the harsh glare of frozen February light from outside blurred the rest of the dim room. She drifted away to that misty time that lived in her memory, that time before she found how cruel life really was.

She was just seventeen, and it was her first Season. Her father and mother were not pushing her to find her husband that year, but the moment she met Hart, then Viscount Eastham, she had known he would be someone special to her. And through the weeks, as they danced and walked and went on carriage rides, she knew what it was to love.

It was late May when she felt the change in him, the more serious intent, the growing maturity. And then, one gorgeous spring day on a carriage ride in the country, he had pulled off into a grove of trees, kissed her gently, and asked her to marry him.

There had never been any doubt of her answer. She was as in love as any seventeen-year-old girl could be, and she said yes immediately. Then came the joy and fervor of planning a wedding, meant to take place at Christmas of that year when their families gathered for the holiday season.

And then, just one week later the horrible fire, the night that lived in her memory as the death of all dreams, happened. She hadn't been there, of course, but she had imagined it a thousand times, the horror, the pain, the fear.

She shook herself out of her reverie. Such a sweet, sad story, their faded love affair. And such a fraud. For when their love was tested, they both crumbled in the face of adversity. Yes, both of them. She had been wrong, but he, too, had shared some small portion of the fault. She would never say that to him, though. It would sound as if she was trying to minimize the pain she had caused, and she would never do that.

She looked at the man now. Was there a way they could have come through it together?

"I hurt you badly, and I am so sorry for it, Hart. The word sorry is too weak." She spoke carefully. "I . . . I am desolate that I hurt you so badly."

"You deserted me the minute I was not your pretty fellow any more," he snapped. "You backed away from me the first time you saw me as if I was . . . as if I were a monster."

She swallowed back a hasty reply, concentrating only on the pain in his voice. She remembered that moment differently. She had come to see him the next day, after the awful fire, and she had recoiled only when he had barked at her to get out, that he did not want to see her. Hadn't she? Or was his memory more accurate than hers?

She had come here to his home to heal the past, not challenge his version of it. She took a deep breath. "I'm sorry, Hart."

"Sorry! What do you know about sorry? You went on with life. I just went on, living, breathing every day, hurting . . . When you sent me that nasty little note I thought I was going to die." He drew back his fist and almost hammered on the glass, but stopped just short.

"You wouldn't see me! What was I supposed to do?" Melony stopped short, biting off her recrimination. She had not come there to argue!

He whirled and glared at her, his scarred face twisted. "You could have been patient. You could have waited! But it was barely a week after the fire when you told me, in that blasted note . . ."

"It was a month, Hart!"

"A . . . a month?" He stopped, arrested in the act of shaking his fist.

"It was a month. Actually a month and almost one week after the fire; do you know how long a month is to a seventeen-year-old girl? It was a full month after the last time I saw you that I . . . I w-wrote the note."

"It was a damnable note. Vile."

"I . . . don't remember what was in it."

"I can quote it for you, every word. You said you feared we would not suit, that you thought . . ."

She shook her head, finally forced to honesty. "I didn't write it."

"What?"

"I didn't write it. Mother wrote it; I just signed my name. I don't even know what she said."

There was silence.

Finally, he said, "You couldn't even be bothered to crush me yourself, you had to have your mother do it?"

"It wasn't like that, it was . . ." She stopped, angry with herself that she had been caught up in recrimination and argument, when she had sworn to herself that was the one thing she would not do. "I didn't come here to fight, Hart."

"Why did you come?"

She crossed to him and boldly stared up into his face. This time he did not shrink back into the shadows; he was too angry. "I came to say I was sorry. I am sorry for all the hurt I put you through." She reached up and touched his scarred face, her fingers tracing the lines of the puckered scars, feeling the hard ridges of scar tissue. He flinched but did not turn away. She felt the tension in him, his whole body quivering as if it was an unbearable strain to hold his position.

"I was so in love with you," he said, his voice trembling with suppressed emotion.

"And I with you."

"But your love didn't last as long as mine did. You ran the first moment there was trouble."

She bit down on her cheek, but at last it would no longer be suppressed. "You *pushed* me away, Hart! You told me you never wanted to see me again!"

"I was in pain! I was grieving. I was horribly injured!"

She put her hands on his shoulders and squeezed. "And I was seventeen and thought it was the end. You *would* not see me anymore, and your mother told me you said I should go, just go away. And my mother said your grief was too great, and you were . . . were a different person. Unable to love. Not in love with me anymore, anyway."

"It doesn't matter, you should have . . ."

"What? Should have what? Waited? Maybe I should have, but seventeen is much more foolish than twenty-eight. I would act differently now, but . . ."

"You would? How?"

She felt his muscles flex and bunch under her hands. A bead of perspiration trickled from his forehead down to his neck and under his shirt. He was an unknown quantity, this Hart she had only just met. He had been a slender, gorgeous youth, romantic, poetic, sweet-natured and gentle, no matter how he wanted to depict his youthful self now. He was no drunken, debauched fellow as he would paint himself. But eleven years and a world of sorrow had changed him. He was hardened with grief and physically changed by years of vigorous outdoor work, Charmian had told her.

He never went to London, content to manage his Staffordshire estate. He had little pleasure in life, and was viewed by most as hard and stern and unrelenting.

"I would make you see me," she whispered, staring at him, willing him to believe her. "If it happened now, I would confront you. I would not let go until you told me to my face you no longer cared."

He was silent. He looked down at her hand on his arm. Some of the tension eased from his body and his muscles relaxed. "If I am to be truthful—and I will honor your honesty with the same, in return—I would have told you to your face what was told to you *for* me. I thought I was dead inside. I knew that part of my life was over and that it would be many years before I . . . before I cared about anything again."

"Oh, Hart," she said. "How you must have missed your father and poor little Lawrence. I remember him, so full of pluck and joy!" She stared at him and saw tears gather in his eyes, spilling out and trickling down his cheek.

She was shocked and horrified when he crumbled, like a great stone battlement crushed by cannon fire. He fell to his knees, sobs shuddering through him and echoing in the great, dim library.

Ten

"Hart!" She fell to her knees in front of him and gathered him to her, feeling him shudder with the great, wracking sobs that still tore through him. The floor was hard under her knees, but physical discomfort disappeared in the pity and compassion she felt for this powerful, commanding man reduced to tears at the memory of his lost family.

And lost youth. For even though he was fully a man when the tragedy occurred, there had been something youthful, even naive about him before the horror that had swallowed him whole. It was lost forever in the fire—his innocence, his joy, his future all burned to cinders, never to be regained.

"I couldn't save them," he gasped. His arms went around her waist and he nuzzled her shoulder as they rocked, his tears soaking thought the delicate fabric of her gown. She felt consumed, swallowed by his great need.

"I couldn't save them," he repeated, sobbing. "I could hear him—my father—I think I even saw them, but then the flames . . . there was a fireball and I was pushed back and the flames overtook me and I . . . I screamed and ran, stumbled. . . . It was horrible. I fell down the stairs, my clothes on fire, my hair . . ."

"Hart," she said, stroking his curls, feeling the sobs

shudder through him. "You almost sacrificed your life trying to save them. You could have done no more!"

"But if I had acted more quickly, if I had not paused . . ."

"Then you would have died in the flames with them and your mother and Lady Charmian would have been left alone."

He stilled and was silent for a long minute. "That's true."

"Of course it's true. And even if it was not, you can't change the past now. That is something I have had to learn through bitter trial."

He sighed deeply and slumped, releasing her, his head bowed. Then he rose from his knees and held out his hand, pulling her to her feet. The tears still gleamed on his cheek, and Melony dried them with the back of her hand. There was awkward silence between them.

He cleared his throat. "Thank you for your kindness," he said, stiffly. He looked down at the floor and frowned, his eyebrows drawing down over his eyes, shadowing his expression, the scarring on his right side puckering. "What did you truly come here for, Melly?"

The old pet name, so casually used, warmed Melony, and yet she could not afford to lose the thread of her thoughts. They had far to go if they were to dispel the ghosts of the past. "May we sit, Hart, and talk?"

His expression cautious, the emotions so recently expressed raw in him—she still could read him sometimes, even though he had changed so over the years—he nodded and indicated a settee by the fireplace.

She sat and waited for him to sit, too, but he paced to the hearth and leaned on the mantel, poking at the empty grate with an iron poker, rubbing off a spot of rust or ash. So he would not bend yet. Well, she had come to make her peace, and for that he need only listen.

"I may have been wrong all those years ago to abandon

you." He was about to speak, but she held up one hand and he fell silent. "I know you have much to say, Hart, and I will gladly listen to whatever you have to say to me on the subject, but please, just hear me for these few minutes."

He nodded and went back to his fiddling.

She patted her skirts down and folded her hands in her lap, gathering her wandering thoughts. It was better if she didn't look at him, for then she was consumed by the memory of being in his arms two nights before. "I find," she started, "that our memories of that time are not completely in agreement, and I did not come here to quarrel about who bore the most wrong. I accept the blame for the pain between us, because it is so true; I should have waited, should have demanded to hear it from you, that all between us was over. So I do not excuse myself."

He remained silent, but the vigor of his actions as he jabbed and poked showed his considerable emotion.

"I visited often, in the first couple of weeks after the fire. Your mother . . . She was so broken, but at first she seemed to be rallying well. I think it had not fully sunk in what she had lost, and so for a while, during your convalescence, she did reasonably well."

He nodded. "It seemed as I healed, she disintegrated before my eyes. When I needed her most she was a tower of strength, but as I got better, she got worse."

"Hart, you have no idea how much I looked forward to having her for a second mother. She was so good, so sweet to me, more so than my own . . ." Stifling a sob, turning it into a cough into her handkerchief, Melony glanced away and summoned the courage to go on. She took in a deep breath. "She was so sad. She said she did not think you would be the same after you healed. I asked to see you, but she said she didn't think it best.

Said it would be too shocking. I think she was trying to protect me."

"From me," he said, ruefully, jabbing at the grate. "It was not just the wounds that would have shocked you. I was bitter, angry, and as I recovered it only got worse." He finally hung the iron on a hook on the hearth and came to sit. "I was fit company for no one. She would not even let Charm sit with me, I was so vile. Absolutely despicable behavior. Go on, please. Do not let me stop you. I will let you speak your piece."

She felt her fingers clutching the fabric of her dress and consciously relaxed her grip. She need only tell him what she came to say, and then she could go home and regain her serenity. This turmoil was hard to bear after the quiet sadness of the past eleven years. And yet coming here was right, she still felt, even knowing now what feelings had been stirred to life by his embrace. It would be a long time before she achieved serenity again.

"I was seventeen," she said. "That month seemed the longest in my life. I cried every night and every morning." She held up a hand as he was about to speak. "I know, I know. It is nothing to your pain. You are absolutely right."

The light dimmed in the room as the February afternoon dwindled and the sun slid down behind the distant midland hills, but Melony felt better in the shadows, just as she had noticed Hart did. "To my young heart the grief felt great enough that I thought I was going to split in two." She clutched her hands to her breast. "In one night everything had changed. I told my mother I would wait for you, however long it took. One day you would turn to me, and I would be there. I sent you a note."

He frowned and shook his head. "I never received any note. Or if I did, I don't remember."

She shrugged. "With both of our mothers gone, who is

to know if it ever left my father's house, and if it did, if your mother thought it was right to worry you with it?"

"Your mother has passed away?" he said, catching her reference to her mother.

Melony nodded. "In November of last year."

"I'm sorry."

"She was ill for over a year; it was a release for her. It is my father who is lost without her now, though I think my brother and his wife may move home to help with the estate. That will be good for Father. I . . . I heard from Charmian that your mother lived only two years after the fire."

He passed one hand over his face, rubbing the corner of his eye where scar tissue puckered the crease. It looked like an habitual action. "Two years to the day. She had faded to a mere wisp, and in the end did not even know Charmian or myself. And yet the doctors could find nothing physically wrong with her."

"I'm so sorry," Melony whispered.

The tension eased out of Hart and he relaxed back on the settee. "It was not an easy time."

"I'm sure it wasn't."

"Charmian has told you much, I understand."

"She has been very good to me."

"And yet when she first wrote, she tells me, it was to castigate you for what you had done to me, in her eyes."

Smiling, Melony recalled receiving the letter. "I was oddly relieved to have someone rail at me. I felt, uneasily, as if a chapter of my life was left unfinished. I had done wrong by you, and it felt good to have someone tell me so. All around me had been telling me for so long that I had had no choice, that it was for the best . . . all that soothing nonsense, but Lady Charmian told me I was selfish and shallow, and it felt like someone had finally spoken the truth out loud, what I had been thinking and feeling for years. As strange as that may seem, it was so."

He frowned and then grimaced. "I do not like ladies arguing over me like that. It is not seemly."

"Charmian loves you. She had a right to say what she said."

"And you answered back?"

"I did. There was so much I wanted to know, and yet I felt I had no right to approach after so many years. Her letter broke through the silence."

"You were just speaking of the note you wrote that I do not remember receiving. What did it say?"

"I asked if I could see you, just to talk. I said that I knew it was early, and that you were still grieving for your father, but that I would like to just sit with you, talk to you, be with you."

"And you heard . . ."

"Nothing. And then, when I visited, your mother said you did not want to see me ever again. She was kind, but firm. I assumed that was in answer to my note."

Hart grimaced, and frowned over at the fireplace. "I . . . I may have told her that. I am not sure now, but I know I was angry at everyone and everything. It is possible I told her to tell you to leave me alone. It's been so long." He glanced over at her. "I have held on to that grudge for a long time. I think . . . something Charmian said to me once is beginning to make sense."

Melony stayed silent, but gazed steadily at him.

"She told me I was holding on to my anger at you so I would not have to be angry at anyone else, all the people who died. I am not sure she is right. After all, what is there to be angry at when my father died rescuing my brother, and my mother died of a broken heart?"

"I'm not so sure that anger, or any other strong emotion, is a completely rational thing, Hart," Melony said, slowly. "We fall in love, after all, long before we can be sure that the person we fall in love with is a suitable partner for life. Anger would have been your way of . . . well, of avoiding destroying yourself."

He shrugged. "Does any of it matter anymore? You have apologized, I have accepted and apologized, in turn, for treating you badly. That is an end."

"Is it all over, Hart? Truly?" She took in a deep breath and sat up straight. She would not go away again with unsaid words, unspoken questions. "If it is all over, then what about two nights ago? What did that mean?"

Eleven

He squinted through the dimness and grunted a reply.

"I didn't hear you," she said, watching his eyes, or what she could see of them.

He got up and paced, and then stood in front of her, looking down at her. "Two nights ago I thought you were someone else. You played a shabby trick on me. Now, in the light of day, it all seems like just a dream."

"But it wasn't. We talked. We . . . kissed."

"I thought you were someone else."

"I am."

Silence, and the sound of a clock tock-tock-tocking away the seconds reminded Melony of the night at the ball, and the sound of the chimes that had ended her fairy tale yet again.

"I almost married, Hart. Did you know that?"

If she had intended to shock him, it worked.

"You *almost* . . . What happened to *that* groom? Did he become scarred and undesirable too?" One second after he said it, he shook his head and passed his hand over his eyes. "I'm sorry. Old habit, to blame you."

"He died at sea," she said, as if he had not spoken. "He wanted to marry before he went, but I did not want to; I wasn't sure. And then he died."

"You have had bad luck with fiancés, haven't you?"

She winced, feeling the shot as he had no doubt intended.

He slumped down next to her, the seat sagging under his considerable weight. "I'm doing it again. I cannot seem to stop being cruel, but I swear I will. I'm sorry, Melony."

She put out a hand blindly, not able to see for the tears, and he grasped it and kissed it. "I loved him in a way, though it was different from how I cared for you. Very different. But he was a nice man, a gentle man, and I would not marry him when he wanted. I didn't think I felt as I ought toward him. I was judging from the past, from *our* love, and that was not fair to poor Richard."

Again, only the sound of the clock on the mantel broke the silence.

"I still don't understand why you did what you did at the ball the other night," he said, keeping hold of her hand and squeezing it. "But I accept you were not trying to hurt me. I can understand curiosity alone could have made you do it."

She let it go. It wasn't curiosity alone, though that had inevitably played a part, but there would, she hoped, be time for explanation later. She was beginning to wonder if there was more between them than she had even hoped. He was transforming before her eyes, changing into the man Charmian had so long claimed in her letters still existed, and who should know but the sister with whom he lived? Charmian said he had moments of black despair, but he valiantly struggled against it, and was ever gentle and considerate with her. When Charmian's fiancé had died on the battlefield at Salamanca, Hart had been the strong shoulder upon which she wept and beat and railed.

That man—that gentle, strong, good, kind man—still lived.

What did that mean for her, though?

"Those first days after the fire must have been so hard for you, Hart," she said. "I wish I had been there for you the way a wife-to-be should have been."

"You were only seventeen, Melly. At twenty-two that did not seem so young to me, but now, at my age, seventeen seems like a child." He caressed her hand, absently, his thumb rubbing her palm.

"To be honest, I *was* frightened, frightened by the tragedy, and frightened by . . . oh, the air of doom that clung to your family. I had been so sheltered that I did not know what to do. I was terrified of . . . of your wounds, too."

"I saw it in your eyes that first day, when you visited me. I saw the fear, but I saw the pity, too, and that was more than I could bear. We did not know then if I would have sight in my right eye, or if I would ever be able to use my arm and hand again, and I kept picturing you, young and beautiful and blooming, tied forever to a hulking cripple. I think that in that moment I decided I would rather have your hatred than your pity. I thought you were summoning up the courage to be the good, compassionate little woman, and I could not stand it."

"Men do not bear up under compassion well," Melony said, her tone dry. "And your sex in general does not seem to understand that if love is real, it transcends the physical, goes far beyond merely a sturdy body and handsome face. Or at least in your youth you judge so." She inched toward him, wanting the comfort of his presence.

He jumped up from the sofa, releasing her hand abruptly. "Uh, it is getting chilly in here. I should light a fire . . . or . . . or tell Charmian to unlock the damned door so you can be on your way now that we have settled the past . . . or . . . I suppose you will stay here the night, now," he finished, glancing out the darkening window.

"Light the fire, first," Melony said, softly, intrigued by his new nervousness around her.

As he knelt on the hearth, she closed the curtains and returned to the settee by the large, baroque-carved fireplace. He got a blaze going and dusted his hands off, rising and stretching. She watched the interplay of muscles under his form-fitting breeches and felt a suffocating wave of heated desire sweep over her. She was no child but a woman now, and understood much more of the attraction between men and women. He had taught her, in their evening together at the ball, just how skilled he was at eliciting passion from her, and she wanted to teach him, in return, that he could feel that same desire for *her,* even knowing who she was.

"Hart, I wish things had been different," she whispered.

"I beg your pardon?"

"Come closer," she said, patting the seat beside her on the sofa.

He appeared to struggle with his decision before succumbing and sitting beside her. She had sat down in the middle of the sofa, so he was, perforce, close to her.

"It has gotten cold now that the room is so dark," she said, moving closer to him.

"I can call Charmian and demand that she let us out. You should have a shawl. Or I can just break down the door since she has, no doubt, convinced all the servants to go along with her harebrained scheme. They answer to her, not to me, but the purpose has been served, has it not? I think we understand the past better now. There is adequate blame to go around, I think, and so we should just leave it in the past."

He spoke rapidly, nervously, more verbose than he ever was and gesticulating.

"I would like to leave all the hurt and pain in the

past." She gazed at his face in the flickering firelight, and then, taking the chance, she reached up and touched his cheek.

Hart closed his eyes, feeling her delicate fingers touch his cheek, his scars, and waiting for her to draw back. But she didn't. He opened his eyes and stared down at her, trying to digest the rapid change in feelings he had undergone in the last couple of hours. From revulsion at her presence, he had moved to toleration, and then to acceptance. Much of his anger toward her had dissolved with the realization that both of them had been laboring under misinformation given by those who thought they were doing the best for their beloved children. And now? Now what?

The scarred cheek was still numb for the most part, but there were areas of sensation, and he could feel the light touch of her fingers bringing life to him, to his old wounds. He watched her eyes and slid his arm around her shoulders, drawing her closer, telling himself it was just to warm her, for she was shivering now from the cold. Or from something. Her head on his shoulder, she looked up at him, closed her eyes, and he did what came naturally.

He kissed her, touching her lips with curiosity now, knowing who she was and wondering what difference it would make in his feelings. Cradling her cheek in his hand, he urged her closer and wound his arm around her back, pulling her closer to his body.

Lips like velvet, and now, without the obstruction of the damned masks from the other night, he could feel the silk of her cheek pressed against his rough skin. The kiss lingered and became two, then three, then countless, like waves crashing against the sand. His arms tightened as his breathing quickened, and he felt her pliant mouth open wider to admit him, to allow him to surge into her, filling her with him as arousal pulsed through his body.

He wanted her, wanted Melony, the girl he had dreamed of for years, the woman he had thought lost to him forever. Far from being lost, she was soft and willing, warm and sensual in his arms, her full bosom pressed against his chest.

What was he doing? And why?

He released her, feeling her sigh against his lips as he let her go and pulled away.

"Hart," she said, her voice breathless, her eyes wide. "My whole life I have been stopped from doing anything rash or bold by timidity. I have spent years running, being scared, frightened of pain, fearful of rejection, afraid of life. But I don't want to do that anymore. I want to take chances, experience whatever there is in my future."

She stopped and he watched her eyes in the flickering firelight. She was frightened now, but of what?

"I still love you, Hart. And I want you. I always have."

Twelve

Incredulous, he stared at her. "You *love* me?" he said, and he heard his own tone, heard the disbelief dripping, and the scorn. He stood, paced to the fireplace and whirled, staring at her through the gloom. "Rather, you are an aging spinster now. I must look good to you, living as you now are on your father's largesse, eh? An earl. My scars don't matter so much now."

He expected fury, but what he got was a nod of understanding. Her eyes were wise, and if there was a hint of pain, she hid it, swallowed it back.

"I thought there was still some left," she said. "Some pain, some old anger and suspicion."

Baffled, he watched her. She met his gaze, calmly. So she would not be provoked. He stared into her eyes, waiting, wondering. When she did not speak again, he broke the silence. "What do you want from me?" he whispered.

"I don't know."

"Why did you . . . What did you hope to gain with your masquerade the other night?"

She tucked her feet up under her, and he noticed she was still shivering. Her lovely eyes were wide, the pupils huge and dark, her lips plump and still moist from his incursions on her mouth. He licked his own lips, beating down his lust and desire for her, trying to find anger and failing. He wanted to return to her side, pull her close, nestle her against him. And forget about all the pain of the past.

But she spoke. "At first I just wanted to talk to you. The idea was to meet you, talk for a moment, and then reveal myself and beg for a few minutes of your time. I needed to correct the past, or at least ask for forgiveness. I have felt for some time I would never let go until I had done those things."

"What changed things?"

"You," she said, simply. "Charmian has told me much about you. You go to these masquerades once a year looking for . . . for love, for want of a better word."

He flinched. "I did not think she knew so much of my . . . my affairs."

"She does, and she understands. I'm not sure why she told me. But when we met, and I felt the power of your . . . seduction turned on me, I knew you had singled me out as a possible candidate for one of your brief affairs. The temptation was great to have the chance to talk to you for a while. I had always known there was a possibility once I revealed myself to you that you would just refuse to speak with me. You could walk away, and there would not be a thing I could do—just as you eventually did at the end of our time together."

He approached and stood over her. "You cannot know I would have done that if you had not tricked me."

"You're right." She reached out and took his hand, squeezing it gently. "I never gave you the chance to be as noble as I believe you are."

He shook his head, rejecting her flattery for what it was, or what it must be, sycophancy. "Leave off, Melony. I have never been noble." He slumped down on the settee next to her again.

She withdrew her hand. He watched her eyes, won-

dering about that strange declaration that she loved him
still and wanted him. Was she playing a game? Had he
been right after all? As a spinster of twenty-eight, suitors would not be plentiful. And he was an earl, not the
richest one in the land, but not wanting for anything, either. His mind told him that was the logical answer, but
his heart—

He was completely off balance, not knowing what to
expect from one moment to the next, and it was a dis-
turbing feeling in his ordered and well planned life. She
had upset his equilibrium, but he could no longer say he
wished she had never come. Perhaps that was most dis-
turbing of all, that knowledge.

"You cannot hide from me, Hart; you cannot hide
who you are. Your friends, the Stauntons, told me much
about you, and you are well thought of in these parts as
a good man, a worthy man. Not every gentleman in
your position is thought of in that way, you know."

They had wandered far afield. Far from wanting to
stay away from the subject, he now wanted to know
more, hear more about her declaration of love. He
moved closer to her and saw her eyes widen, but not
with fear or hesitation. He slid his arm over the carved
back of the sofa and his breathing quickened. His desire
warred with his fear; she said she wanted him. How
much? And in what way?

She touched his face again and he closed his eyes,
letting the fear wash through him and releasing it. It
took steely determination not to flinch, not to shy away
from her. Blindly, he leaned in and their lips met. He
sank into her, his head swimming, his brain refusing
all thought but that he was most incredibly aware of
every detail of her, from the way her lush body cradled him to the velvet touch of her lips. She was so
soft and he so hard; it was a meeting of elements, her

moist welcome and his fiery need. She quenched him, swallowed him . . . saved him from incineration.

Lost in sweet delirium, time moved on. Without conscious thought, he lowered her to the settee and they lay together, kissing and touching. He was adrift, alone with her on an island where there were only the two of them. He became inured to fear: fear of what she was really thinking, fear that she was engaged in some deep, devious game, fear of rejection. And yet he knew that for all that, he still admitted the possibility she was toying with him. What did he know of her, after all?

And so he asked her. Holding her close, looking deep into her eyes, their prone position familiar from lovers through the years, he asked her about the last eleven years and how she had coped.

They talked; she talked about her fiancé, a family friend she had loved, but, she saw now, as a friend, not a lover. And he talked about his mother and Charmian, and about the last few years when he had begun to think he was going to descend into his dotage alone and angry, bitter . . . desolate.

"Oh, Hart, Charmian has told me there have been women—good women—who have loved you, but whom you could not love in return." She gazed up at him, cradling his face in her hands. "Love is risk. I am so sorry I hurt you all those years ago."

He shrugged. "Charmian has been telling me lately that I whine. I think I agree with her now. Life cannot be lived without some pain, but it doesn't give us the right to close up like a clamshell and then complain about the loneliness." He shook his head and there was a rueful expression on his face. "I don't know how she's put up with me. I've been selfish and foolish. I think I have been . . . confused as to the pain. You hurt me, but I see that I was just as much to blame. I pushed you away. You were only seventeen; what else could you do but what you did? What more would any woman do, even a more experienced one? I told you to go away. But the pain I felt, it was mostly to do with losing Father and Lawrence. It just hurt less to be angry than to be sad."

Melony's heart ached for him, and she enveloped him in her arms and pulled him down to lay on her breast, his solid weight a comfort. She closed her eyes, but then was startled by the feel of his lips touching her neck, her shoulders, her bosom. His strong hands pulled her closer until she was lying almost under him, his leg thrown over her as he tucked her close to his powerful body. Her stomach churned once more with a wave of yearning, the need to yield to him, to give him everything she could in the short time they would have together before she must go home.

And so she surrendered control to him, feeling all the tension slip away and offering herself to him, but not with words and not with actions. She gave herself over to sensation, to his hands roaming her body, his lips touching her skin, leaving trails of flame and heat, and all the points of contact between them, his broad chest squashing her breasts and pushing the air from her lungs, the feel of his hardness thrust against her hip and his lean, muscular leg thrown across her possessively.

He felt the moment of surrender, felt all the tautness of muscles bunched drain from her as she yielded to his need, to his desire. To his love.

Had he ever stopped loving her? Was it not her ideal spirit that kept him from loving any other woman, just as much as his pain and anguish?

"Melly, did you mean what you said?" He propped himself up on his elbow and gazed down at her, the warm light of the fire dancing across her plump cheeks and lighting her blue eyes. He smoothed back her tangled tresses and gazed steadily into her eyes, seeing no evasion and now, no fear. This was his Valentine dream, he realized, this woman lying beneath him, with him. It had been her voice, her scent, and the memory of lilacs in the rain from their first spring together, so long ago now.

She did not need to ask what, of all they had spoken of that evening, he meant. "I did. I do. I love you Hart. And I want you," she whispered.

It was a confession and a surrender. He gathered her into his arms and kissed her, and for the first time she felt not only his passion, but something else, something eternal and—

Behind them the door lock clattered and the door squeaked open. As Charmian stole into the room, Melony awoke from her dream of rediscovered love to see Hart staggering to his feet. She looked up and saw his sister, and, feeling her face flush a fiery red, she stumbled to her feet, too.

"Go away, Charm," Hart said, grinning. His breathing was heavy and his eyes glittered, but he was smiling hugely.

She frowned and stared at them both. "Why? What is . . ."

"Just . . ." He crossed the floor quickly and whispered to her, and her eyes widened.

"Really?" she squealed, gazing at him wide-eyed.

"I hope so," he said. "Now go," he finished, turning her toward the door and giving her a gentle push. "Go away for a while longer. And feel free to lock us in again."

When she left, the key indeed turning in the lock, he turned back to Melony. He approached her diffidently, and pushed her to sit down on the sofa. He knelt at her feet.

Melony's stomach clenched with fear, fear that what

she hoped and prayed so fervently for was *not* what he intended to say.

He took her hands in his and gazed up at her. "Melly, you've seen how I can be. I can be brooding, gloomy, distrustful. Knowing all that, seeing me as I am today, scarred, past my prime, full of doubt, can you still love me?"

"I don't think I ever stopped. Love has nothing to do with strength or a smooth cheek or a youthful body. I love you, Hart, and did from the beginning for . . . for how vulnerable I knew you were, how you could be hurt. And for your strength inside." She laid her hand on his chest and struggled for the words to express her deepest feelings. "For the power of your heart."

"I never thought I would say this, never believed it could happen, and with you! But it's true. Melly, I love you. Will you marry me at long last?"

In answer, she dropped to her knees on the floor beside him and slid her arms around his waist. He pulled her close.

"Yes . . . oh, yes! I'll love you forever, Hart."

He touched her lips, feeling her whisper her love against them, and his dreams melted into this reality, this woman in his arms and the words of love and forgiveness and reliance that had pulled them together. From now on, their Valentine dreams would all be dreamed together, forever.

Discover The Magic of
Romance With
Jo Goodman

Embrace the Romances of
Shannon Drake

More Zebra Regency Romances